Love Encounters

SULTRY TALES OF LOVE & PASSION

VOLUME 1

EMILY EDWARDS

FREE REIGN

ISBN 13: 978-1-953462-84-8

Free Reign Publishing, LLC
San Diego, CA

Contents

Chapter One

TROPICAL PASSION

As the sun kissed my skin, casting a golden glow over the pristine sandy beach, I reveled in the freedom of my solo vacation. I had always embraced my independent spirit, relishing in the adventure and self-discovery that came with it. With the sound of crashing waves serenading my senses, I basked in the anticipation of the unknown.

The beach stretched before me like a canvas of desire, the soft sand inviting me to sink my toes into its warmth. The rhythmic crashing of waves echoed in harmony with the pounding of my heart, creating a symphony of anticipation. The cerulean expanse of the ocean stretched as far as the eye could see, it mirrored the secrets and depths of my own desires. The salty breeze carried the scent of adventure while the sky above was adorned with fluffy white clouds, adding a touch of innocence to the scene below. The sun was casting its golden rays upon the beach, imbuing everything with a warm glow. It was here, amidst the allure of sand and sea, that my journey into the realms of passion and sensuality would unfold.

As I walked along the shoreline, the gentle waves lapped at my feet, leaving a trail of cool wetness in their wake. Seashells, scattered like precious gems, whispered stories of hidden treasures and forgotten secrets. The beach was a playground for lovers and dreamers alike, its embrace offering a sanctuary where inhibitions could be shed and desires explored. The warm sand caressed my bare skin, leaving a tingling sensation in its wake. Nature itself was whispering sweet nothings into my ear. It was a place where time lost its grip, allowing moments to stretch and merge, creating a space where fantasies could materialize, and passions could ignite.

I walked to the Tiki Bar and sat down, enjoying the warm breeze, and ordered a mojito. After getting my drink, I decided to stay at the bar and repositioned myself so I would be in alignment with the setting sun.

It was there I first saw him. He emerged from the shoreline like a Greek god carved from marble, his sun-kissed skin glistening with droplets of seawater. The sand clung to him, accentuating the contours of his chiseled chest and sculpted abs, as if nature herself couldn't resist the temptation to leave its mark upon his magnificent form.

With each step, his muscles flexed, creating a hypnotic rhythm that sent a surge of heat coursing through my veins. His presence was magnetic, drawing me closer with an irresistible force that defied reason. As my eyes traced the trail of sand dusting across his chest, I couldn't help but imagine the sensual journey my fingertips could embark upon, tracing the lines and curves of his sculpted body. I found myself wanting to dust him off, slowly.

He exuded an aura of raw masculinity, a potent blend of strength and confidence that left me breathless and yearning for more. His smoldering gaze met mine, filled with a mix of mischief and desire that set my senses ablaze. It was a look that spoke volumes, igniting a fire deep within me that I never knew existed.

His lips, full and enticing, curled into a seductive smirk that promised a world of pleasures. The stubble on his jawline hinted at the raw, untamed nature that lay beneath his composed exterior. I could almost taste the hint of salt lingering on his skin, a testament to the strength that radiated from every pore of his being. His presence alone was a temptation, a delicious invitation to surrender to the wild, primal desires that surged through me. In that moment, I knew I wanted to embark on a journey of unrivaled intensity, guided by the touch of his hands and the fire in his eyes.

He walked over to the bar and sat next to me. Keeping his eyes fixed on the bar top, he reached for the nuts that were in the bowl in front of me. His large hand slid inside my bowl. He picked up a few and popped them into the back of his mouth. I couldn't figure out why he was eating out of my bowl when there was one directly in front of him.

"Aloha" he said, nodding in the bartender's direction. He must be a regular, I thought. The bartender walked over and poured a tall glass of water for him. That's what he was, one tall drink of water.

The tropical breeze caressed my skin, reminding me how long it had been since I had been touched by a man. The boundaries of propriety and caution blurred, consumed by an irresistible longing. The forbidden allure of our connection beckoned me, daring me to abandon reason and surrender to the intoxicating spell.

The chemistry between us was a smoldering inferno, a fusion of heat and electricity that crackled in the air. Even the thought of a fleeting touch sent shivers of anticipation coursing through my body. His aura brushed against my body. My skin ignited a wildfire of desire, leaving me trembling in his wake. Somehow I knew, our bodies were magnetically drawn to one another and down inside, I yearned for the electrifying connection. There was an invisible force that pulled me closer to him, at least in spirit, fueling the hunger that burned deep within. In the Tiki Bar of Desire, I only wanted to be intertwined in a steamy bout of passion. I wanted to intertwine with this god of the sea and find a rhythm that only he could satisfy.

He sat there, drinking his water in silence and eating my nuts. When the bowl of nuts had been consumed, he spoke, asking if I was going to the luau tonight. I told him I had just gotten to the island and I wasn't sure.

His voice, a low, velvet whisper, sent a shiver down my spine as he leaned in, his breath teasing my earlobe. "Meet me here tonight," he murmured, his words dripping with seduction and promise. Each syllable was laced with a magnetic allure that left me weak in the knees, my pulse quickening with anticipation. His voice alone aroused me, painting vivid images of the intoxicating encounters living in my wildest dreams. The invitation hung in the air like an unspoken agreement, an invitation to surrender to the depths of our desires under the moonlit sky. With that simple command, he stoked the flames of anticipation within me, fueling the fantasies that played out in my mind with a tantalizing intensity. A surge of heat coursed through me, leaving no doubt that tonight, our encounter would be nothing short of unfor-gettable.

I nodded yes. Yes, I would be here. I began sipping on my straw, imagining other things, and smiled that Mona Lisa smile of mine, cutting my eyes up at him. He nodded and pushed back the chair, stood and returned to his home world of the sea. Aquatic gods must do that, I thought. Come ashore and find human women, then take them to their underwater castle. I was sure that was how it happened.

Leaving the beach behind, I made my way back to my room, my mind buzzing with a heady mix of excitement and anticipation. The thought of the upcoming luau, with its vibrant colors, swaying hips, oh, the swaying of hips, and sultry rhythms, fueled my imagination. I slipped out of my bikini, relishing the touch of the fabric against my bare skin as I chose a dress that clung to my curves, hinting at the desires that simmered within. I adorned myself with delicate jewelry, each piece a whisper of sensuality against my flesh. With a final glance in the mirror, I embraced the confident goddess that stared back at me and returned to the moonlit beach to meet the Sea God.

I walked toward the sound of the crashing waves and emerged from the shadows, the glow of torches cast a trop-ical and magical light upon his sculpted form. The Sea God stood at the water's edge, his gaze fixed upon me as if I were the ocean's most alluring treasure. The flickering flames danced across his skin, accentuating the contours of his powerful physique, while the moonlight painted a silvery halo around him. His eyes sparkled with a mischievous glimmer, mirroring the fire that burned within my own depths. With each step towards him, the excitement coursed through me, a symphony of desire resounding in my veins. In that moment, as our eyes locked, the world faded away, leaving only the pulsating energy between us, a magnetic pull that drew me closer to the Sea God, where our destinies would intertwine in a dance of passion and pleasure.

He wasn't much of a conversationalist, but I was sure he made up for that in other areas.

In the soft glow of the moonlight, he closed the distance between us with a purposeful stride, his eyes smoldering with desire. As he reached me, time stopped, and without a word, he swept me into his arms with a strength that both surprised and thrilled me. My heart raced as he held me close, his touch igniting a fire within me that demanded release. In that embrace, our bodies melded together, fitting perfectly as if we were two halves of a passionate equation. And then, his lips met mine with a hunger that matched my own, a kiss that spoke of longing, of pent-up desires finally set free. He kissed me the way I deserved to be kissed, with a fervor that ignited every nerve ending, leaving me breathless and craving more.

With one arm he lifted me, carrying me effortlessly. He whisked me away from the moonlit beach, the sand giving way to a path that led to his private cabana. The night air caressed my skin as he carried me, each step filling me with anticipation for the secrets that awaited us. The warm glow of candles danced in the dimly lit space, casting shadows that played upon our bodies as he gently laid me down on a plush, inviting bed. His eyes never left mine as he hovered above me, the air thick with electricity. In that instant I knew that tonight my needs would not be met by the Cabana Boy. Tonight my desires would be met by the *Cabana Man*.

As his hands roamed my body, tracing the contours of my skin with an expertise that left me trembling, a heat surged within me. Our bodies moved in perfect harmony, fueled by a shared hunger that consumed us both. His touch was both gentle and demanding, his fingertips leaving trails of fire in their wake. With each caress, a symphony of moans and whispered gasps filled the air, a testament to the pleasure we unleashed in one another. Our lips met in a passionate dance, tongues exploring and mingling, the taste of desire merging with the saltiness of the sea. In that moment, our bodies connected and the world around us dissolved into a haze of pleasure and ecstasy.

I emerged from his arms, aware that I was now on Island Time. Only our desires mattered. I was propelled to new heights of pleasure, ones I never knew existed. I surrendered to the depths of his touch. In that sacred space, we abandoned ourselves to the primal desires that surged within.

I began to get up and leave the web I was in, but his hands possessively gripped my hips and pulled me back to him. All I knew was that it must be high tide. Waves of pleasure continued to crash over me for the rest of the night, an intoxicating rush that threatened to drown me in its embrace. The air was thick with a heady mixture of sweat, desire, and the raw essence of our union.

The universe seemed to hold its breath as we reacted to each other. It only makes since the universe would wait. He was a Sea God after all. As our connection transcended the physical and we joined the Etherial Plane, we collapsed into each other's arms, bodies entwined and souls entangled. We had ventured into a realm of unbridled passion and desire, a realm where our deepest longings were met and fulfilled.

In the depths of our passionate encounter, I discovered true liberation by surrendering to my desires. In embracing the intensity of our connection, I shed the confines of inhibitions and societal expectations. With each gasp, each moan that escaped my lips, I shed layers of self-doubt and reservation. I realized that to truly experience the richness of life, I needed to surrender to the wild, untamed desires that coursed through me.

By embracing the fire that burned within, I set myself free from the chains of judgment and self-restraint. In the moment of our intimate union, I found liberation in the raw vulnerability that came with exposing my deepest desires. It was through the exploration of pleasure, the embrace of my sensual self, that I discovered a profound sense of self-acceptance and empowerment. I learned that true liberation lies in honoring the desires that whisper within, and in surrendering to the intoxicating dance of passion, I set myself free to experience life's most exquisite pleasures.

I was able to let go of the need to please others and instead focused on my own needs and desires. It was a powerful act of self-love and self-discovery, where I found the courage to indulge in the depths of pleasure without guilt or shame. By surrendering to desire, I embraced a newfound authenticity, celebrating the raw, passionate being that lay deep within.

By surrendering to desire, I had liberated my soul, allowing it to soar on the wings of passion and self-discovery. I had unlocked a part of myself that had long been suppressed, embracing the fullness of my desires and embracing the beauty of my sensual nature. It was in that liberation that I found a deeper connection to my own essence, and a renewed zest for life itself.

Gazing upon the Sea God, his body peacefully asleep, I felt a surge of admiration mixed with a tinge of bittersweet longing. The moonlight bathed his sculpted form, casting gentle shadows across his features, highlighting the depth of his allure. As I watched him slumber, a smile played at the corners of my lips, but deep within, a realization stirred - a desire to reclaim my independence and rediscover the essence of who I am.

Leaving the Sea God behind, I made my way into the night, my steps confident and purposeful. It wasn't a walk of shame, but rather a walk of self-empowerment, a journey to reconnect with the fire that burned within me. Each stride held a subtle sway of my hips, a reminder of the sensual power that resided within my very being. In the darkness, under the moon's watchful gaze, I embraced the freedom of my own desires, eager to explore the uncharted territories that lay ahead.

With every step I took, a renewed sense of liberation coursed through my veins. The night air whispered secrets, urging me to shed the remnants of the past and embrace the possibilities that awaited me. It was a walk of rediscovery, a journey to reclaim my true self. The memories of our encounter lingered like a tantalizing perfume, mingling with the thrill of newfound independence. In that moment, I realized that my sensual awakening was not confined to one night, but rather the catalyst for a larger transformation - an exploration of my desires, passions, and the boundless pleasures that awaited me on the path of self-discovery.

Chapter Two

THE VLOGGER

I lived in a world that revolved around screens and lines of code. Virtual realms were my solace, where I found refuge from the tumultuous nature of human connections. Love had eluded me, leaving behind the bitter taste of heartache and disappointment. It seemed that my destiny was to live a solitary existence, alone with my faithful feline companion, Tobe. Together, we created our own cocoon, where the soft purrs and gentle nuzzles provided a semblance of companionship.

I had given up on the idea of finding a love that could penetrate the barriers I had erected around my heart, surrendering to the belief that my happiness could be found within the embrace of solitude. Each day I would pray the winds of change would blow life into my world, but by the end of the night I realized I was in an El Nino dry heat pattern.

It was a serendipitous click, a mere flicker of curiosity that led me to stumble upon his vlog. From the very first video, I was transfixed, spellbound by the enigmatic vlogger who effortlessly wove tales of adventure and laughter. Each word that escaped his lips resonated deep within my soul, as if he were whispering secrets meant only for me. Night after night, I found myself perched in the darkness, like a silent observer, peering into his world through the luminescent glow of my screen. I became a willing voyeur, living vicariously through his daring escapades, feeling the rush of adrenaline and the caress of new experiences.

With every upload, he breathed life into my monotonous existence, filling the voids with his vibrant energy and contagious zest for life. I was no longer a mere spectator; I was an accomplice in his adventures, silently cheering him on, yearning to step out from the shadows and join him in his quest for the extraordinary.

Months passed like fleeting seasons, the vlogger's presence becoming an inseparable part of my daily routine. Each video brought a surge of emotions, and with every passing day, my desire to connect with him grew stronger. Yet, the struggle that waged within me was relentless, as doubts and insecurities clouded my judgment. Should I dare to disturb the delicate balance of his online world? Would my words be met with indifference or rejection? The fear of being dismissed or considered an intruder gnawed at my resolve. But deep within my heart, a flicker of bravery ignited, urging me to break free from the chains of self-doubt.

Summoning every ounce of courage, I sat down to write that fateful message, my fingers hovering hesitantly over the keyboard. In that moment, I chose to confront my fears, believing that even the smallest chance at connection was worth the risk of vulnerability. With trembling fingers, I carefully crafted each word of the message, pouring my hopes and dreams into its virtual embrace. Every sentence was a delicate dance of vulnerability and authenticity, baring a piece of my soul to a stranger who had become so much more.

Nervousness coursed through my veins like a tempest, my heart pounding against the confines of my chest. Doubts clawed at the edges of my mind, questioning the audacity of my gesture. Would he see through the carefully constructed facade of my life? Would he understand the depth of my longing, the yearning that had taken root within me? I felt like a tightrope walker, teetering on the thin rope of possibility and uncertainty, acutely aware of the weight of my choice. I was willing to take this chance for him; I was willing to fall.

As I read and reread my message, a kaleidoscope of emotions swirled within me. Hope mingled with fear, intertwining like two dancers locked in a graceful yet dangerous waltz. My senses were on overdrive with the possibility of a connection that transcended the boundaries of a digital world. I felt an inexplicable pull, a magnetic force drawing me towards the vlogger. In that moment, I surrendered to the tide of emotions, allowing myself to revel in the intoxicating cocktail of longing, excitement, and vulnerability.

With a deep breath, I closed my eyes and summoned all the courage I had. The weight of my anticipation bore down upon me, making my every breath a conscious effort. But in that moment, I made a choice. I chose to believe in the power of connection, to trust that vulnerability could lead to something beautiful. I moved my trembling finger and pressed the send button, relinquishing my carefully crafted message into the vast expanse of the digital realm. In that single click, I sent forth a piece of my soul hoping for the possibility that it would reach the vlogger's heart and bridge the gap between us.

Within a few short hours, a notification flickered on my screen, signaling a response from the vlogger. My heart skipped a beat as I eagerly opened the message, my eyes scanning each word with a mix of disbelief and elation. I couldn't believe it. He had taken the time to read my message and had responded with genuine warmth and interest. In that moment, I realized that the invisible threads that had connected us through the ethernet were growing stronger, weaving a tapestry of connection and possibility.

As our conversation unfolded, we delved deeper into our shared interests and values, like two puzzle pieces seamlessly fitting together. Each message exchanged revealed hidden layers of our personalities, fostering a sense of understanding and kinship. Our conversations danced between lighthearted banter and soul-stirring discussions. We spoke of dreams and ambitions, of fears and triumphs, peeling away the layers of our protective shells and revealed the vulnerable hearts beating within us. In those virtual encounters bond began to form, transcending the boundaries of pixels and screens.

Through our exchanges, a connection and understanding slowly unfurled. It was like switching from SD to HD. It was the first time I saw the clarity of the world. Shared laughter and reflections became the foundation of our friendship. We discovered that despite the physical distance between us, our minds could intertwine and bridge the gap that separated our lives. His words resonated deep within me and as our connection grew, I couldn't help but wonder if this digital encounter held the potential for something more - something that could cross the boundary of the matrix and connect our destinies.

Our messages grew into a world of intimate interfacings. With each exchange of words, our connection grew stronger. We delved beyond the surface, exploring the depths of our pasts, fears, and joys. Our words danced in a synchronicity that defied logic. In those letters, I found a confidant, a kindred spirit with whom I could share my deepest secrets and desires. With each heartfelt message, our bond grew, nurturing the seed of affection that had sprouted in the fertile ground of our virtual connection.

Time passed and our virtual connection continued to flourish. And then, one day, he suggested we meet in person. I stared at the blinking cursor, my heart caught between exhilaration and trepidation. The mere thought of bridging the gap between our digital lives and stepping into the realm of reality sent waves of uncertainty crashing over me. What should I say? How should I respond? My mind swirled with a kaleidoscope of emotions, each one vying for dominance. Fear mingled with anticipation, as I grappled with the enormity of this moment.

I wanted to see him, to feel the warmth of his presence, to look into his eyes and know if the connection we shared transcended the confines of our virtual encounters. Yet, in that moment, I could only stare at the cursor, at a loss for words that could capture the depth of my conflicted heart.

Weeks stretched before me like an eternity, each day marked by a mix of excitement and nervous anticipation. I counted down the hours, minutes, and seconds until the moment our virtual connection would transform into tangible reality. My world shifted, like a dream transitioning into wakefulness, as the cyber fantasy we had woven together slowly gave way to the vast expanse of the real world. And then, the day arrived - the day we were to meet on the North Rim of the Grand Canyon, a place that held promises of adventure and breathtaking beauty.

As I stood at the edge of the majestic canyon, my heart thrumming with a heady mix of exhilaration and apprehension, I couldn't help but marvel at the magic of the world wide web that had brought us together. This was no ordinary meeting; it was the merging of two souls who had journeyed a virtual landscape, navigating emotions and forged a connection that had defied the boundaries of distance. The grandeur of the high desert stretched before us, an awe-inspiring backdrop for the adventure that awaited. We set out to explore, hiking along Bright Angel trail, our footsteps echoing in harmony with our shared laughter. With each step, my doubts lifted, replaced by a sense of belonging, as if we had been chosen to discover the magic of the rim together.

In the high desert, amidst the towering cliffs and breathtaking vistas, our connection deepened and flourished. I marveled at the ginormous pine trees and the play of sunlight on the ancient rocks of the canyon. We shared secrets and whispered dreams as we sat under a sky ablaze with stars. The North Rim was already a sacred space, and even more so now. It is a land where our virtual encounters merged seamlessly with the tangibility of the world around us. Together, we began to memories and etched our beings into the fabric of this vast and timeless landscape. In those moments, I realized that what had once been a flickering screen had become the foundation of a love story, forever entwined amidst the grandeur of nature and the whispers of our shared hearts.

As the evening sky painted hues of amber and gold, the last ember of the fire barely hung on. Tony carefully extinguished the campfire, his hands moving with a practiced ease. The crackling flames gave way to a gentle wisp of smoke, blending into the starlit canvas above. We stood in the embrace of the night, the crisp air carrying the scent of pine and earth. The dancing shadows cast by the dying embers flickered across our faces, bidding us goodnight. With a satisfied smile, Tony turned towards me, his eyes sparkling with a mixture of adventure and tenderness. It was time to retire for the night, to seek refuge in the cozy confines of the small log cabin that awaited us on the edge of the rim.

Hand in hand, we made our way towards the cabin, our steps quiet against the earthy path. The cabin stood as a sanctuary, a haven amidst the grandeur of nature. Its weathered logs and rustic charm welcomed us with open arms. Inside, a warm glow bathed the space, emanating from the crackling fireplace. The air was infused with a sense of tranquility, inviting us to unwind and surrender to the lullaby of the wilderness. As we settled into the comfort of the cabin, a sense of peace settled with us. It was time to bid the day farewell, to let our bodies find each other, and to dream of the adventures that awaited us.

Tony's touch sent shivers cascading down my spine as he took my hand and guided me toward the inviting expanse of the bed. The air crackled and the room seemed to hum with an electric charge. The bed beckoned, adorned with a thick patchwork quilt that held the essence of the cabin's rustic charm. Its rich colors and intricate stitching mirrored the layers of desire that wrapped us in that moment. I traced my fingers over the fabric, feeling the warmth and softness beneath my touch, as if the quilt itself held the secrets of countless passionate nights that had unfolded within these walls.

"Flip it back", I asked. He didn't understand at first. I asked again, "flip it back". Tony was brave and adventurous, but I wanted nothing to do with any black widow spider who might be nesting beneath the blankets. That was beyond the limit of my adventure.

He laughed, flipping back all the blankets and satisfying my curiosity.

Then, with a tantalizing slowness, Tony's hands traced the contours of my body as he gently pulled my shirt over my head. The touch of his fingertips sent an electric current coursing through my veins, awakening every nerve ending to a heightened state of awareness. The room seemed to hold its breath. As the fabric slipped away, revealing the curves and valleys of my skin, a rush of heat flooded my senses. Time stood still in that moment, suspended in a dance of desire and vulnerability. His touch ignited a symphony of sensations, like a brushstroke of fire against my bare flesh, setting every inch of my being ablaze with an exquisite ache for more.

With a gentle yet confident pull, Tony drew me closer, our bodies now mere inches apart. He created a burning intensity, reflecting the fire that blazed within me. Time stood still as we embraced, our lips tasting the intoxicating blend of longing and surrender. The room was awash with the glow of the fireplace, casting shadows that mirrored the ebb and flow of our desire. In that moment, the cabin became a haven of sensuality, a place where the boundaries between reality and fantasy blurred, and where our souls at last intertwined in a passionate dance.

As we sank into the quilt, its plushness cradled us, amplifying the intimacy of our connection. Each thread, each stitch, held the weight of our desires, and wove us together in a tapestry of pleasure. The quilt whispered of past lovers who had sought refuge beneath its layers, igniting a flame that burned through the night. Our bodies melded and we reveled in the exploration of each other's desires. The softness of the quilt against my skin heightened every sensation, and I yearned for more.

Time lost all meaning as we succumbed to the ardor that pulsed between us. The room became a sanctuary of shared vulnerability and raw passion. Our bodies moved with a synchronicity born from an intimate understanding, each touch and kiss a language only we could decipher. The connection surrounded us, building like a crescendo, until we were consumed by the sheer intensity of our desires. In that moment, the boundaries of the world dissolved.

As the embers of our passion slowly subsided, we lay tangled within the quilt's embrace, our bodies glistening with the remnants of our shared fervor. The room was hushed, save for the echoes of our ragged breaths. We remained locked in a silent embrace, our hearts beating in rhythm, as the patchwork quilt whispered tales of love and desire that had unfolded beneath its comforting layers. In that bed, in that cabin on the edge of the rim, we had created a moment of sublime connection, a memory that would remain forever etched upon my soul.

In the depths of passion, we surrendered to the rhythm that pulsed between us, our bodies locked in a passionate embrace. Time stopped as we explored the depths of our desires, each touch and caress a symphony of pleasure. Our lips danced in a fervent ballet, sharing whispered promises and pleasurable sighs. The room became a stage, where our bodies moved as one, lost in a sensual dance that left us breathless, wanting more.

As the night deepened, the intensity of our connection soared, each moment building upon the last. The passion ignited a fire that blazed through the darkness. We reveled in the exquisite torment of our passions, indulging in the basic instincts that guided us. The room was awash with the symphony of moans and gasps, a sweet harmony of pleasure that filled every corner. We were consumed by the sheer power of our love, surrendering to the heady whirl-wind of ecstasy that swept us away.

With the first gentle hues of dawn beginning to paint the sky, we collapsed in a breathless heap, our bodies spent, yet still yearning for the touch of one another. Our shared sighs mingled with the soft light that filtered through the window. In that moment, as the world outside stirred to life, we clung to each other, hearts beating in synchrony, knowing that the night we had shared would forever stay in the deepest recesses of our souls.

After only a few precious hours of sleep, we stirred reluctantly, our souls still drunk on the intoxication of our love. With heavy hearts and aching limbs, we gathered our backpacks, feeling the weight of the inevitable departure settling upon us. The night, brimming with whispered promises and stolen moments, had come to an end, and the dawn demanded our return to reality.

As I stood at the rim of the canyon, I could only look at the breathtaking vista before me. Tony approached with a quiet grace. His presence surrounded me in a tender embrace. Taking my shoulders in his hands, he turned me to face him, his eyes filled with a mixture of longing and tenderness. In that moment, time stood still again, ageless against the backdrop of the Grand Canyon. Our lips met in a bittersweet kiss, filled with the echoes of our shared desires. The taste of him lingered on my lips, mingling with the ancient breeze that swept through the canyon.

With our hearts pounding in unison, he pulled away slightly, his voice a soft murmur against my skin. "Same time, next year?" he whispered, his words carrying a weight of hope and uncertainty. The question hung in the air, pregnant with possibilities and the unspoken yearning to keep the flame of our connection alive. In that fleeting moment, our shared desires and the realization of the outside world colliding with our private sanctuary, I found solace in his arms. And with a gentle smile, I responded, "Yes, same time, next year," sealing our shared secret, our clandestine vow to rekindle the passion that had ignited between us on this sacred ground.

Chapter Three

THE TRAIN

I stepped onto the crowded train, my heart pounding with anticipation. The day had been a whirlwind of meetings and deadlines, leaving me yearning for a moment of rest. As luck would have it, the only available seat was next to a captivating stranger. His smoldering gaze met mine, and a flicker of soul recognition passed between us.

"Oh, sorry, this is my stop", he said and quickly rose and left the train. Life was cruel that way, taking away a man of mystery so quickly. But in that moment that I knew, without a doubt, that fate had orchestrated this encounter, weaving our paths together. Whatever the reason, I knew that the circumstances of our meeting were no accident, but rather a testament to the intoxicating power of fate and desire intertwining.

In the days that followed, I found myself hopelessly entangled in thoughts of the mysterious stranger. The mere memory of his touch awakened desires that had remained dormant inside me far too long. His presence had unlocked a hidden side of myself, one that craved the thrill of forbidden seduction. Perhaps it was the shared loneliness in his gaze, the unspoken stories etched in the lines of his face, that called to the wild and untamed corners of my own heart.

You don't meet someone and fall instantly for them. And we didn't even speak! The memory of the stranger, once so vivid and intoxicating, started to fade like a wispy dream upon waking. Doubt gnawed at my insides, whispering cruel words that perhaps it was all a figment of my overactive imagination. I wondered if I had conjured up an affair of the heart that existed only in the depths of my despair.

Night after night, I would retreat to the solace of my dreams, hoping to reunite with the stranger in the ethereal realm of fantasy. But even there, the flame of passion dimmed, unable to sustain the fiery intensity that once burned so brightly. The imaginary affair had reached its expiration date, leaving me with a hollow ache in the wake of its dissolution. I longed for the touch, the whispered promises, and the stolen moments that now seemed like distant echoes of a forbidden love. It became increasingly clear that I had built castles in the air, crafted an illusion that my heart yearned to believe, but that reality refused to embrace.

Two months had slipped away since my encounter with the mysterious stranger, and life had resumed its steady rhythm. I was resigned to the notion that our paths would never cross again, the encounter was something my psyche created to fill the void in my life. I decided to throw my passions into my work instead and started seeking a creative project in the city.

Within weeks I had an offer to supervise the art instillation for a new building. I was being beckoned to the bustling city where dreams were born and destinies were interlaced. Excited, I prepared for the new chapter that awaited, my heart fluttering with the anticipation of the unknown.

Dressed in my alpha-woman attire, I made my way to the train station, my steps infused with a renewed sense of purpose. The platform teemed with a sea of faces, each lost in their own world of ambitions and desires. And then, I saw him. There, amidst the crowd, stood the stranger, his captivating gaze finding mine with a magnetic pull that defied all logic. My heart skipped a beat as he too approached the platform, his presence setting the air ablaze with an electric charge. With every inch he drew closer, my breath quickened, and I dared to believe that fate had once again brought us together.

The stranger moved with a grace that mirrored that of a prowling lion, each step purposeful and fluid. His body seemed to glide through the world effortlessly, as if he had mastered the art of traversing life's obstacles with a regal poise. He possessed an innate understanding of his own physicality, a primal confidence that emanated from within. The way he carried himself exuded an aura of dominance, as if he were the king of his own realm.

His hair, a tousled mane of dark waves, accentuated the chiseled contours of his face. It framed his features with an almost magnetic allure, drawing attention to his piercing eyes and strong jawline. His hair mirrored the untamed spirit that resided within him, a reflection of the wild passions that simmered beneath the surface. With every movement, his hair danced with the rhythm of his steps, adding an air of mystery and untamed allure.

There was no doubt in my mind that he must be a Leo. He possessed the essence of the lion - the confidence, the power, and the magnetic presence that commanded attention without uttering a single word. Just like the zodiac sign, he exuded warmth and charisma, effortlessly captivating those around him. The fire that burned within his soul was evident in every gesture, every glance, as if he were destined to leave an indelible mark on the world. And in that moment, as I found myself drawn deeper into his elliptical orbit, I couldn't help but wonder if I would be caught in the irresistible pull of his celestial charm.

I was thankful at this moment that I had studied astrology. As a Libra, I found myself grateful for the balance and harmony that defined my nature. On the surface, I appeared business-like and composed. But beneath the upper layer, there was a world, a secret part of me, that reveled in expressing my inner sensuality. Beneath the polished exterior, I delighted in my own desires. It was my personal descent, a clandestine rebellion, against the boundaries imposed by the outside world.

Hidden beneath the elegance of my dress, I adorned myself with black lace, a whisper of seduction against my skin. Delicate patterns intertwined, tracing a sensual dance across my curves, revealing glimpses of a hidden passion that yearned to be set free. The intricate fabric clung to me like a lover's touch, reminding me of the enchantment that lay beneath the surface. It was my little secret, a reminder that I was not defined solely by the rigid structures of the male-dominated world but by the untamed desires that resided within me. In the moments when I felt the lace against my skin, I felt a surge of empowerment, knowing that beneath the façade, a world of untamed passion awaited.

My heart quickened at the sight of the stranger. Taking

this as a good sign, I knew this day was going to be one I would always remember. I became distracted in his eyes again, and for a moment I lost track of time. Looking at my phone to check the hour, I saw the train starting to board. Quickly, I navigated through the crowd and boarded the train just in time. Breathing a sigh of relief, I made my way down the narrow aisle, my eyes darting from one seat to another in hopes of finding an empty spot.

To my dismay, the only available seat was tucked away in the back of the train, far from the prying eyes of the world. As the train started to move, I settled into the seat, feeling a mixture of disappointment and gratitude. Disappointment that I wouldn't have a chance to catch a glimpse of the stranger, but gratitude that no one had claimed the empty seats around me. It provided a small sanctuary, a momentary breath where I could indulge in some much-needed solitude.

In the secluded haven of the back of the train, I allowed myself to relax and savor the tranquility. It was a rare moment of peace amidst the chaos of everyday life, a chance to steal some precious "me" time. As the world outside whizzed by, I closed my eyes, letting the rhythmic motion of the train lull me into a state of tranquility. It was a moment of surrender, a temporary escape from the demands and expectations that weighed upon my shoulders. Here, in the peaceful embrace of the train, I could let go, if only for a little while, and immerse myself in the sanctuary of my own thoughts.

As the train rumbled to life, the world outside gradually blurred into a mesmerizing tapestry of lights and shadows. The familiar sights of the station dissolved into a hazy backdrop as the train gained momentum, carrying me further away from the realm of ordinary existence. The dimming of the lights within the car allowed me to relax a bit further.

Lost in the trance of the passing scenery, I found myself gazing out the window, not really seeing, my eyes fixed upon the blur of colors and shapes that whirled by. The rhythmic clatter of the train wheels seemed to sync with the beating of my heart. I knew I was not in control of this journey. I was being aligned with my fate.

And then, as if summoned by the mystical forces that governed fate, I looked up and there, standing before me, was the stranger. He asked if he could join me and joked about this being the only seat left.

Time paused in that moment as our eyes locked, the air thick with an unspoken recognition. With deliberate grace, he moved closer, taking the seat beside me. A jolt shot through me, a delicious mixture of thrill and trepidation. The world had shrunk to encompass only the two of us, cocooning us in an intimate bubble in the back of the train. In that suspended moment, I felt the thread that connected our souls.

The intoxicating scent of his cologne enveloped me, its seductive musky notes filling the air and stirring a primal desire. It was a fragrance that spoke of confidence and sensuality, a potent elixir that intoxicated my senses. The subtle interplay of scents mingled with the rhythm of the train, creating an irresistible allure that drew me closer, inch by tantalizing inch.

As he settled into the seat beside me, I could feel the warmth radiating from his body, seeping through the fabric that separated us. It was a comforting heat, a tangible connection that sparked a whirlwind of emotions within me. I found myself torn between the thrill of the unknown and the caution of propriety, unsure of how to navigate the uncharted territory that lay before me. Every fiber of my being yearned to lean into the magnetism between us, to explore the unspoken desires that flickered in his eyes. But a part of me hesitated, held back by the fear of crossing boundaries and the uncertainty of what lay ahead.

In that suspended moment, I was adrift in a sea of conflicting emotions. The chemistry that crackled between us was undeniable, but I grappled with the question of what I should do next. Should I surrender to the intoxicating pull of his presence, or should I retreat to the safety of familiarity? All I knew was that in his proximity, my world had shifted irreversibly, and I stood on the precipice of a choice that would redefine everything.

Crossing my legs, a soft whisper of the nylon stockings I wore beneath my skirt peeked out, a subtle hint of seduction that escaped the confines of my composed facade. In a reflexive motion, I smoothed my skirt back down, my face flushed with a mixture of embarrassment and a thrilling awareness of his gaze upon me. I couldn't help but steal a timid glance at him, my heart fluttering with anticipation.

To my delight he was smiling, a spark of excitement illuminating his eyes. He had caught the subtle invitation hidden in the flutter of my dark lashes and the delicate revelation of my nylons. In that moment, I knew we were both eager participants in this dance of temptation. There was a heady mixture of attraction and unspoken desires that warped around us like a magnetic field. With each sway of the train and the subtle brush of our arms, the tension grew. I was not a meteorologist, but I knew that any connection would unleash a storm of passion.

I became aroused with the knowledge that he too was affected by this intoxicating chemistry. It emboldened me, stirring a newfound confidence within my soul. With a shy yet playful smile, I met his eyes, acknowledging the cosmic pull that had brought us together. The anticipation in his gaze mirrored my own, fueling a fire that blazed beneath the surface.

"Hi. I'm Randy. I mean, my *name* is Randy," he said, his voice a velvety timbre. As the words left his lips, he extended his hand toward me, a silent invitation to bridge the gap between us. His hand, warm and strong, hovered before me.

I felt the weight of a decision pressing upon my heart. It was a simple gesture, a handshake, but it held within it the power to bridge the divide between strangers. With a fluttering pulse and a racing mind, I reached out and placed my hand in his, allowing our fingers to finally meet. In that moment of contact, a current surged between us. I felt the walls I had built around my heart begin to crumble. In his eyes, I saw mirrored reflections of my desire.

I chose to play it safe, steering our conversation toward lighthearted small talk as the train continued its rhythmic journey. For the next hour, we spoke of inconsequential matters, our words skimming the surface of our thoughts.

As we exchanged stories and anecdotes, I found out more about him. He shared with me the devastating loss of his fiancée, a tragedy that had left him shattered and seeking solace in the embrace of work. It was through his career that he sought to fill the void, burying his grief beneath the demands and distractions of his profession. I thought that in my pursuit of success, I had become a master at masking pain, but clearly he was the winner.

As the train came to a halt, the jarring interruption pulled us back to the reality of our surroundings. With a soft sigh, he turned towards me, gratitude shining in his eyes. "Thank you for listening," he said, his voice laced with a hint of vulnerability. It was a fleeting moment, as he quickly gathered his belongings and made his way towards the exit. There was an unspoken understanding that our encounter was but a fleeting connection. I watched him fade into the crowd, carrying his burdened heart and secret sorrows, leaving me with a bittersweet longing for a future that would never be.

I gathered my belongings and prepared myself for the bustling city that awaited me. The train had brought me to the start of a new chapter, a chance to reclaim my place in the working world. I was to meet the owner of a Fortune 500 Company. This was the key to my professional revival. Excitement mingled with nerves, my heart pounding with anticipation as I envisioned the possibilities that lay before me. This meeting, this opportunity, held the promise of a fresh start, a chance to showcase my skills and reignite the passion that had died within me. With renewed determination, I stepped off the train, ready to embrace the challenges and triumphs that awaited me in the vibrant tapestry of the city.

Thoughts of Randy lingered in the recesses of my mind, his presence still palpable even as I embarked on this new professional journey. The memory of our encounter played like a haunting melody in the depths of my soul. I hailed a cab and slid into the backseat, my focus shifted to the task at hand. The job, the opportunity that lay ahead, became my singular purpose.

The cab whisked through the bustling streets, skyscrapers rising like sentinels around me, casting long shadows that mirrored the uncertainties and possibilities that awaited. The memory of Randy's captivating presence flickered in my mind like a distant star, a temptation I dared not indulge in, at least not now. Squaring my shoulders, I felt the touch of the black lace on my skin and I was a filled with surge of empowerment. I was going to knock this job out of the park. I mentally prepared myself to make an impression on the owner, hoping he'd like my work so much he'd invite me to work for him full-time. In this moment, my focus was steadfast, my mind committed to seizing this opportunity and breathing life back into my career.

The cab came to a halt, and I stepped out onto the bustling sidewalk. With a quick adjustment, I smoothed the fabric of my skirt. This moment, this step onto the solid ground, marked the beginning of a new life for me. I could feel it in the depths of my being. I stood solid, knowing that whatever was behind those doors secretly whispered my destiny.

As I approached the impressive building, determination coursed through my veins. I reaffirmed my commitment to embrace this opportunity, to leave behind the shadows of the past and forge a path towards a brighter future. Pulling open the door to the grand lobby, I stepped into a space brimming with energy and possibility. I knew that I had arrived at the threshold of the future, ready to seize the challenges and triumphs that awaited me within these walls.

With a confident stride, I approached the reception desk. "I'm here to meet Mr. Clarkson," I stated, my voice steady and determined. She nodded with a polite smile, directing me towards a group of men gathered at the foot of the grand staircase. Architects, designers, investors, businessmen. It was a sight that captured attention; I could feel the power radiating from their presence.

I made my way over to the distinguished group. Standing at the back of the group, I caught one man's attention. He nodded, indicating he wanted to know what i needed. I politely asked for Mr. Clarkson, explaining that I was here for a meeting. With those words, a tall figure turned around, eyes still fixated on the brown journal in his hand. "I'm Mr. Clarkson".

The tall figure turned around, his commanding presence instantly capturing the attention of everyone around him. Clad in a tailored suit that accentuated his powerful physique, he wore a hard hat in a manner that suggested a seamless blend of authority and rugged charm.

He turned to face me and a jolt of recognition shot through my veins, leaving me breathless with disbelief. "I'm Randy Clarkson," he said as he turned. His eyes sparkled with a glimmer of recognition, and a warm smile curved his lips as he extended his hand towards me. Our eyes locked, a mixture of surprise and recognition passing between us. I accepted his gesture, our hands met in a firm yet gentle grasp, a familiar current passed between us. In that simple touch, a flood of emotions surged through me, reaffirming the connection we had shared on that train journey. The universe had brought us together once more.

I realized that our paths had converged not by chance but by an invisible force, guiding us towards a future that held the promise of profound connection and undeniable passion. Fate had brought us together once again, not as fleeting strangers on a train, but as two individuals bound by the intertwined threads of our lives. Little did I know that this encounter would mark the beginning of a journey far beyond my wildest imagination.

Chapter Four

WORDS OF PASSION

The brisk autumn breeze danced playfully through the vibrant leaves as I strolled along the cobblestone streets of the enchanting town of Willowbrook. As a passionate writer, I sought inspiration in every corner of this picturesque haven. Little did I know that fate had conspired to gift me an encounter that would forever change the course of my life.

It was in the cozy corner of an intimate café that our paths intertwined. My eyes were drawn to a mysterious figure seated alone, his gaze fixed upon the pages of a worn leather-bound notebook. His ink-stained fingers glided gracefully across the page, bringing his thoughts to life. Intrigued by his creativity, I found myself inexplicably drawn to him.

He exuded an aura of mystery, his presence

commanding attention without uttering a single word. Dressed in a tailored charcoal gray suit that hugged his form in all the right places, he exuded an air of refined confidence that sent shivers down my spine. His tousled chestnut hair fell in disarray, lending him an irresistible charm that whispered of passionate nights filled with unbridled desire. The cologne he wore evoked a feeling of primal lust, wakening the woman that I had hidden.

Every movement of his was deliberate, every gesture laced with an undercurrent of restrained power. His presence filled the room, magnetic and impossible to resist. There was an undeniable allure in the way he carried himself, a combination of grace and raw masculinity that had me yearning to unravel the mysteries that lay beneath that impeccably tailored suit.

From beneath the sweep of his dark lashes, his piercing blue eyes met mine, a glimmer of untamed sensuality shimmering within their depths. I was sure they held secrets, longings that begged to be unraveled, and I couldn't help but be captivated by the hidden depths they promised to reveal. His strong jawline hinted at a strength of character that left no room for doubt - this was a man who knew what he wanted, and he pursued it with fervor.

As I dared to approach him, my gaze traveled downward, drinking in the sight of his broad shoulders that tapered to a slim waist. My eyes drifted over, making sure his left hand was unencumbered from any gold band.

Curiosity whispered in my ear, urging me to seize the opportunity. Summoning every ounce of courage within me, I willed my legs to carry me toward him. With a graceful stride, I approached his table, feeling the warmth of anticipation and nervousness intertwine within me. As I stood before him, my voice quivered slightly as I introduced myself, the words slipping from my lips like a delicate melody. He looked up, his gaze meeting mine with a mixture of curiosity and intrigue, and a flicker of a smile danced at the corners of his lips. It was in that moment, as our eyes locked, that I knew destiny had brought us together, and our entwined journey was about to unfold, page by tantalizing page.

His name was Adrian McCoy, a renowned novelist known for his evocative storytelling. Our shared love for literature created an instant connection, like two pens dipping into a common ink well, we were destined to write the most passionate of tales together.

Hours slipped away like fleeting moments, stolen from the clutches of time itself. The soft glow of candlelight caressed our features, casting a seductive glow upon our bodies. The café was closing its doors, signaling the end of this enchanting encounter. With a mixture of reluctance and anticipation, Adrian leaned closer, his voice a low, velvety whisper that ignited flames of longing within me.

"Can we meet again, same time tomorrow?" he asked, his words lingering in the air like a promise yet to be fulfilled. The invitation, laden with unspoken desires, sent shivers down my spine, evoking a hunger that could only be sated by the touch of his lips and the exploration of his passionate embrace. With a nod and a glimmer of mischief in my eyes, I accepted, knowing that our next meeting would unlock a world of untamed ecstasy, where the lines between fiction and reality would blur, and our words would become the brushstrokes that painted our bodies with fervent desire.

Our encounters became frequent, and as we delved into each other's lives, our stories mixed like intricate plot lines. Adrian's words were intoxicating, his voice as smoother than velvet, which made my heart race and my palms tingle with anticipation. He spoke of distant lands and unrequited love, while I shared my own stories of triumph and heartbreak.

Adrian's heart, though adorned with the laurels of literary acclaim, bore the deep scars of unrequited love. He had loved fiercely, pouring his emotions into the words that graced his novels, yet his affections had remained unreciprocated. The echoes of past heartbreaks whispered in the recesses of his soul, shaping him into a man whose tender vulnerability lay just beneath the surface. It was within the confines of his unfulfilled desires that his stories were birthed, intertwining the realms of fiction and reality, and it was in his quest for a love that matched the intensity of his own that he had stumbled upon the path that led us to this moment of destiny. The atmosphere of the cafe transformed into an ethereal haven for forbidden desires. His eyes, echoing a cloudless sky of blue sparkled with an unspoken invitation. I felt the electricity in the air as our fingertips brushed, kindling a flame of undeniable attraction.

In only a matter of days, and nights, our desires blossomed like the words on the pages of our shared stories. Each touch, each caress, held a thousand promises, weaving a tapestry of sensuality. The warmth of his lips against mine was like a sonnet written just for us, and as our bodies entwined, our souls danced a passionate waltz.

In the realm of our own creation, time ceased to exist. Adrian's touch awakened a sensuality within me, each stroke of his hand across my skin igniting a symphony of pleasure that resonated deep within my core.

As the night wrapped us in its embrace, my fingertips yearned to trace the contours of Adrian's flesh, to map the secret worlds hidden within the expanse of his skin. Every brush of my touch ignited a symphony of sensations, each caress a whispered promise of pleasure yet to come. I longed to feel the heat of his body melding with mine, to intertwine our limbs in a passionate tangle where time would stand still, and only the rhythm of our desire would dictate the tempo.

We were alone in his cabin. With each stolen glance and the faintest brush of our bodies, the hunger between us intensified, a relentless craving that pulsed in time with our racing hearts. The allure of his form, sculpted with masculine perfection, beckoned me like a siren's call, urging me to explore the depths of his passion. I yearned to taste the salt-sweetness of his skin, to leave my mark upon him, and to feel his sighs of pleasure mingle with my own as we melted into one another, two souls united in a storm of carnal bliss. The anticipation hung in the air, thick with desire, as we danced on the precipice of ecstasy, ready to succumb to the inevitable union that would render us breathless and forever bound by the electric current of our love.

A tremor coursed through me as Adrian's hand, warm and daring, slipped beneath the fabric of my shirt, igniting a trail of goosebumps in its wake. His touch, both gentle and possessive, traced the contours of my skin, his finger-tips whispering secrets that sent shivers of anticipation dancing along my spine. In that stolen moment, our desires melded into a symphony of longing, and I surrendered to the intoxicating pull of his embrace.

With a surge of primal strength, Adrian effortlessly scooped me up into his arms, his muscles flexing with a raw power that only fueled the fire of our desire. The world spun, the room a blur of sensuous hues, as I found myself suspended in his embrace, weightless and consumed by the sheer intensity of our connection. In that moment, I felt the undeniable strength of his desire, the unspoken promise of a passion that would take us to dizzying heights. As he held me aloft, our bodies fused together, I knew that I had found not only a lover but a partner who would carry me to realms of pleasure I had only dreamt of.

As dawn painted the sky with hues of rose and gold, I found myself nestled against Adrian's chest, our bodies sated and entwined in a tender embrace. The morning light cascaded through the parted curtains, its gentle touch caressed our entwined bodies, illuminating the aftermath of our passionate union. A soft haze of contentment enveloped us, our limbs still entangled, as if reluctant to release the tangible evidence of our desires awakened. I reveled in the delicate ache that lingered within, a lingering reminder of the exquisite pleasure we had shared, a tapestry woven from the threads of our heated connection.

With every rise and fall of our chests, the room hummed with the residual energy of our lovemaking. The air held a heady mixture of our scents, mingling and intertwining in an intoxicating symphony that permeated our senses. We basked in the afterglow, our bodies bathed in the soft hues of morning, as if the very sun itself sought to pay homage to the passion that had consumed us throughout the night.

In that quiet sanctuary of tangled sheets and tangled limbs, our desires lay exposed, stripped of all pretense. We had awakened a primal yearning within each other, a hunger that could never be quenched. It was as if a dormant fire had been stoked to life, forever burning with an intensity that would drive us to explore new realms of pleasure, where the boundaries of our desires would be pushed and surpassed. In that hallowed space, we reveled in the knowledge that we had discovered a love that surpassed all expectations, a love that would forever leave its mark upon our souls.

In the sanctuary of Adrian's arms, I found peace and fulfillment beyond measure. The allure of his touch, the way his body melded with mine, was a revelation. It was as if our bodies had been sculpted to fit perfectly together, igniting a hunger that only he could satisfy. In those moments, time ceased to exist, and I knew with unwavering certainty that I never wanted to leave the shadow of his embrace.

Our connection went beyond the physical; it infused our writing, becoming the catalyst for a new level of creativity. Adrian's words, fueled by our shared intimacy, took on a newfound depth and passion. We became each other's muse, inspiring tales of desire and longing that transcended the realms of fiction. Our lovemaking became research in its purest form, an exploration of the intricacies of pleasure and the depths of human connection. Each touch, each whisper, became a study in sensuality, painting vivid strokes of inspiration across the canvas of our shared stories.

In those moments of passion, I delved into the heart of our desires, peeling back the layers of vulnerability and exposing the rawest essence of our beings. The lines between reality and fantasy blurred, as I lived out the most explicit scenes with an abandon reserved only for those who had found their true counterpart. Our bodies became the vessels of our research, the intimate dance of flesh and desire providing a wellspring of inspiration that flowed freely onto the pages of my novels. In the depths of our exploration, I discovered a creative synergy that transcended words, for it was in the heat of our connection that my stories found their truest form.

In the years that followed, my love continued to bloom, our shared passion for storytelling mirrored in the tapestry of our lives. I became a conductor; words danced across pages, capturing the essence of love, forever immortalized in the annals of literature.

In this embrace, I discovered the true magic of storytelling - a power that could transport souls, ignite desires, and bind two hearts as one. Within the written word lies an alchemical power, a force that can ignite flames of passion, transcend the boundaries of reality, and forge connections that defy logic. The inked strokes on a page possess the ability to awaken dormant desires, to evoke emotions buried deep within the recesses of the soul. Through the written word, passion finds its voice, its tendrils entwining with the reader's desire and imagination, creating a symphony of yearning and surrender. It is in the dance between writer and reader, where desires are laid bare and shared, that the true magic of literature resides - a testament to the intoxicating fusion of passion and the written word, forever entwined the dance of seduction.

Chapter Five

THE BRIDGE

I still remember the day the letters started arriving. It was a crisp autumn morning when I unlocked the door to my quaint little bookstore, greeted by a bundle of mail on the counter.

I had been working at the charming bookstore nestled on the corner of a quiet street. Inside a world of enchantment was held within its walls. As I unlocked the door each morning, a symphony of creaking floorboards and the soft scent of aged paper greeted me, evoking a sense of nostalgia and literary magic. Sunlight filtered through the small windows as I opened the shades, casting a warm glow on the rows of bookshelves, lined with treasures waiting to be discovered. The air was filled with a gentle hush, as if the books whispered their stories to one another, eager to be shared with those who wandered through their pages.

The cozy reading nooks, adorned with worn armchairs and soft blankets, invited visitors to lose themselves in the realms of imagination, while the aroma of freshly brewed coffee from the small café corner enticed them to linger a little longer. It was a sanctuary for book lovers, a haven where words came alive, and where I found a safehouse amidst the pages of countless stories.

On that day, the day the first letter arrived, the world was adorned with hues of amber and gold. I found myself standing in the doorway of my bookstore, the cool breeze gently brushing against my cheeks. I was only taking a moment, a moment to enjoy the day. I saw regular customers walking towards me and I turned to go back inside. I walked behind the counter and began to sort the mail, stopping when I noticed a letter that was addressed to me.

With anticipation trembling in my fingertips, I carefully extracted the letter from its companions. The paper was textured, bearing a subtle cream hue that whispered of age and history. Its edges, torn by hand with deliberate care, gave it a touch of whimsical authenticity. I marveled at the elegance of the handwriting adorning the envelope, each stroke revealing the writer's meticulous attention to detail. My breath caught in my throat as my eyes traced the curves and loops of my name, a handwritten address that held the promise of something extraordinary.

Running my hand over the delicate paper, I felt a faint tingle of excitement, as if the secret contained within could only be unlocked by the gentle touch of my fingertips. The crispness of the autumn air mirrored the crispness of the paper, and I found myself lost in a moment suspended in time. The universe had conspired to orchestrate this encounter, this dance between my fingers and the words yet to be unveiled. With a mixture of curiosity and trepidation, I carried the letter closer to my heart, ready to embark on a journey that would forever change the trajectory of my life.

Soon I found that every morning, as the sun gently filtered through the sheer curtains of my bedroom, I would descend the stairs with eager anticipation, hoping another love letter awaited me. The delicate scent of fresh ink and the smooth texture of the paper beckoned me closer, urging me to unfold the secrets that lay within. With each letter, the words unfolded like petals, revealing a profound longing and a deep understanding of the depths of my soul. They painted vivid pictures of love, of stolen glances and whispered promises, leaving me breathless and yearning for more.

As I read those letters, time stood still. The outside world faded into insignificance, and I became immersed in the realm of heartfelt emotions and lyrical expressions. The words danced across the page, serenading my heart with their enchanting melody. They held me captive, like a lover's hand caressing my skin, leaving traces of longing and anticipation in their wake. Each carefully crafted sentence resonated within me, creating a symphony of emotions that resonated through my very being.

Those letters made me feel alive. They awakened a dormant passion within, igniting a fire that had long been extinguished. The words painted vibrant hues on the canvas of my heart, evoking emotions I thought were long lost. I could almost feel the warmth of his touch, his voice whispering in my ear. They became the rhythm of my days, the pulse that quickened my heartbeat, reminding me of the boundless possibilities of love. They were too perfect. I felt as if I shared them with anyone the magical spell would be broken so I kept them to myself.

Days turned into weeks, and the mystery of the letters deepened. I found myself lost in a minotaur's maze of possibilities, questioning the identity of the writer who had managed to captivate my heart so effortlessly. Was it someone I knew, someone who had witnessed my quiet moments of vulnerability? Or was it a customer from the bookstore, someone who had observed my passions and yearnings from afar?

I carefully studied the letters, dissecting each word like a detective examining clues at a crime scene. I analyzed the handwriting, searching for familiar strokes or peculiarities that might unveil the writer's identity. I observed the book-store visitors, watching for telltale signs of recognition or hidden glances that might betray a connection. The daily interactions with the patrons took on a new dimension as I scrutinized their every move, desperately seeking any hint of familiarity.

Friends and acquaintances were not spared from my inquiries. I engaged them in conversations about the art of letter-writing, subtly probing for insights into their own experiences or inclinations. I listened intently to their stories, hoping to stumble upon a confession or a slip of the tongue that would expose the secret sender. Yet, as the days passed and the list of potential authors grew, the truth seemed to slip further from my grasp, leaving me with nothing but a bewildering array of possibilities.

The letters had become a source of both delight and frustration, teasing me with their anonymity. Each word held a spark of familiarity, a glimpse of a connection that danced at the edge of my consciousness. And so, I continued my quest, my determination fueled by equal parts curiosity and longing. With each passing day, I yearned to unravel the mystery, to uncover the face behind the words that had woven their way into the fabric of my heart.

The letters breathed life into a romance that existed beyond the confines of screens and instant gratification.

With each letter, the writer revealed fragments of his soul, crafting a love story that transcended time and space. Those letters became my lifeline, a lifeline that tugged at my heartstrings, reminding me that love could still be found in the most unexpected of ways. I found myself falling in between the lines, deeper into the romance that stretched across the pages.

In the midst of my search for the sender, the letters became a sanctuary, a source of comfort and hope. I was wrapped in a warm embrace, whispered promises of a love that knew no boundaries. With every stroke of the pen, a tapestry of emotions touched the depths of my being. And as I held each letter close to my heart, I knew that love had found a way to bridge the distance between us, one word at a time. I felt like each day I opened a new chapter of life, the letters reminiscent of the love poems of Browning. *I love thee to the depth and breadth and height my soul can reach...* My mystery lover was perfect. And if I never searched for him he would remain that way to me forever - perfect.

The words, woven together with eloquence, awakened a sense of curiosity and longing within my soul. I found myself eagerly anticipating each new arrival, the anticipation mounting with every step towards the mailbox. My heart grew so full, I had to share with someone or I knew it would burst. I decided to confide in my close friend,

Emma. She encouraged me to uncover the identity of the secret admirer who had found a way to touch my heart so deeply. Emma, always having my well-being at heart, cautioned me; what if this a is twisted joke?

I had never thought of that. How could someone be so cruel? What if this was all a clever ruse, a practical joke designed to toy with my emotions? The idea that the letters might be nothing more than an elaborate facade, woven to deceive and amuse, casted a shadow over the excitement that had filled my heart. A pang of vulnerability pierced through me as I contemplated the possibility of being the unwitting victim of an intricate prank. The delicate paper in my hands suddenly felt heavy, as doubts whispered their insidious questions, challenging the authenticity of the emotions kindled by those mysterious letters. I began to fill ill, swooning for a moment but catching myself before I fell. I felt the need to sit for a moment. Try and find my breath. Could someone be so sick, so twisted? How could someone even think about doing a heinous crime such as this? Before falling any deeper, I need to know who the mysterious sender was. Armed with determination and a touch of apprehension, I began my quest for the truth.

The first suspect was Henry, a tall and handsome gentleman who frequently visited the bookstore. His charming smile and friendly nature made him an ideal candidate. However, as I observed his interactions and analyzed the letters, I couldn't quite match the words to his personality. I knew in my soul he was not the sender and so the hunt continued.

A few days later, amidst the stacks of books, I noticed Ethan. He was a regular customer, quiet and unassuming, often seen lost in the pages of a novel. There was an air of mystery surrounding him, a quality that intrigued me. Was he the enigmatic writer of those letters? As I stole glances in his direction, I couldn't help but notice the subtle shift in his demeanor whenever our eyes met.

One evening, as the sun began to set, Ethan approached the counter with a book in hand. We engaged in a conversation that ventured beyond the usual pleasantries, delving into our shared love for literature. The connection between us grew stronger, and with each passing moment, I wondered if he was the one. But the doubt remained, nestled deep within my heart.

The letters continued to arrive. The emotions they evoked grew more profound, and my desire to uncover the sender's identity intensified. The contents of the letters ignited a fire within me that I had long forgotten. Each carefully chosen word, each passionate phrase, fueled desires I had kept locked away. At first, I blushed, feeling a sense of embarrassment wash over me as the writer unveiled his intimate thoughts and desires with such unabashed vulnerability. But as I delved deeper into the letters, a longing stirred within my soul, craving the touch of the writer, the taste of his lips, and the embrace of his arms.

The writer's words painted vivid scenes of stolen moments in hidden alcoves, whispered confessions in the moonlit night, and fiery passions that consumed our beings. With each letter, the boundaries of propriety melted away, leaving me yearning for the forbidden, for a love that defied societal norms. The letters possessed a magnetic pull, drawing me closer to a realm of sensual delights and untamed passion. In the solitude of my thoughts, I found myself surrendering to the vivid fantasies woven by the writer's skilled hand.

My cheeks flushed, my heart raced, and I dared to admit that I longed for the writer, not just physically, but to caress his soul, to intertwine our desires and vulnerabilities in a dance of unparalleled intimacy. The words woke a hunger within me, a yearning to explore the depths of passion and surrender myself to the tempestuous whirlwind of love. No longer did I feel embarrassment or shame, for those letters had awakened desires that had slumbered for far too long. I craved the touch, the presence, and the essence of the writer, my heart aching to experience the intoxicating blend of love and desire that his words promised.

Night after night, as I read the tantalizing letters over and over, a familiar routine began to unfold. With each word that stirred my deepest desires, I found myself retreating to the solace of my bedroom, the letters clutched tightly in my hand. There, in the privacy of my own sanctuary, I surrendered to the intoxicating power of the writer's words. With each stroke of my fingertips against my skin, I sought to satiate the longing that pulsed within me, imagining the writer's hands exploring every inch of my body with the same passion and intensity that flowed from his pen. In those stolen moments of pleasure, I wondered if he knew the profound effect he had on me, if he could feel the electricity that surged through my veins as I surrendered to his seductive prose.

As the nights unfolded, my imagination took flight, carrying me to a realm where reality blurred with fantasy. I wondered what it would be like if we were to meet, if the sparks that ignited within the confines of those letters could manifest into something tangible, something that transcended the boundaries of ink and paper. Would the chemistry we shared through his words translate into a palpable connection? Would the intensity that coursed through his correspondence be replicated in the touch of our bodies? The yearning grew stronger, the craving to experience the depths of passion and connection that the writer had evoked within me. It was an unquenchable desire, an ache that demanded to be sated, leaving me longing for a reality where the writer and I could come together and merge our worlds in a collision of desires and shared intimacy.

I wanted the writer. I craved his soul. He was all I could think about, day and night. I was fixated on finding him.

Yet, amidst the search, a blossoming friendship had developed between Ethan and me. Our conversations became a source of peace, a refuge from the turmoil of uncertainty. Fate had intertwined our paths, making it harder for me to fathom a life without him. The letters created a storm of emotions in my life and I soon found that Ethan was the calm in my storm.

On a cold winter's night, as snowflakes danced outside the window of the bookstore, Ethan and I found ourselves alone. With hesitant voices, we spoke of our fears and vulnerabilities, our hearts laid bare before one another. It was in that moment that I realized our connection was deeper than any words written in those letters. It was a connection that transcended the mystery.

And then, in the midst of my revelation, a truth unveiled itself. Ethan, with a mixture of nervousness and tenderness in his eyes, confessed his love for me. The enigmatic letters were his creation, his way of capturing my attention and igniting a spark between us.

Oh, the relief and joy that flooded my heart when I discovered that it was Ethan, my dear Ethan, who had been the mastermind behind those bewitching letters all along. The realization that the love we had cultivated through his written words could now find expression in this tangible world brought an indescribable sense of elation. No longer confined to the realms of fantasy, our love could flourish in the sunlight, breathing life into our shared dreams and desires. The letters had served as a bridge, connecting our souls across the distance, and now, with Ethan by my side, our love story could continue to unfold in the most beautiful of ways.

As we embarked on this new chapter of our lives, our love grew with a fervor that surpassed even the passion depicted in those captivating letters. The touch of Ethan's hand against mine sent electric currents coursing through my veins, each caress a testament to the depth of our connection. The conversation, once limited to ink and paper, now danced upon the air, filled with laughter, whispered promises, and shared dreams. The love that had blossomed within the confines of his written words now manifested itself in the passionate taste of his lips against mine, the warmth of his embrace, and the comfort of his presence.

In this newfound togetherness, Ethan and I realized that the love we had nurtured through the letters was just the beginning of a grand love story that continued to unfold with each passing day. The challenges we faced and the obstacles we overcame only deepened our bond, strengthening our commitment to one another. The intimacy I discovered through his words now intertwined with the physical and emotional connection we shared, creating a tapestry of love that was both breathtaking and profound. With Ethan by my side, I knew that our love story would be etched upon the annals of time, a testament to the enduring power of love, the magic of the written word, and the serendipitous beauty of two souls finding their way to each other.

PUBLISHER'S EXCERPT

STALKED: TERRIFYING TRUE CRIME STORIES:
VOLUME 1

BAD SUSHI SAVED MY LIFE

This incident had happened to me in the fall of 2009. I had just been through a rough break up and needed my alone time more than ever. I never imagined that my relationship with Mark would end up this way. We had started off so full of hope and love. But as with most over time, his true colors began to emerge. The charming and caring man I fell for slowly transformed into a manipulative and emotionally abusive partner.

It took me a long time to realize that I was in a relationship with a narcissist. The constant gaslighting, the belittling comments, and the control he exerted over every aspect of my life had chipped away at my self-esteem. He had taken control of my funds, my access to my family and even found a way to get people to spy on me. After a few years I came to the realization that I had become a shell of the person I once was. I had become lost in the web of his manipulation.

But one day, I found the strength to break free. He had been talking to other girls about leaving me and how little I truly mattered to him. The worst part of it is that he told other people that I was the abuser not him. That broke me. The person I had fallen for was long dead. I gathered the shattered pieces of my heart and made the difficult decision to end things with Mark. Little did I know that he would react in such a harsh and unexpected way.

Shortly after our breakup, Mark's behavior became increasingly erratic. He would send me long, rambling messages filled with anger and resentment. He accused me of ruining his life and vowed to make me pay for leaving him. He would show up at my work or church just standing or sitting there staring at me for sometimes hours. More than once I had to be walked back to my car by fellow employees. I would find flowers and notes of love and apology or (on the bad days) Hateful notes calling me names. Once I came out to having flat tires. It was clear that he was spiraling out of control. I tried to tell his family, but I thought it had fallen on deaf ears.

Then came the news that Mark had been admitted to a mental ward in a hospital about an hour away. I couldn't help but feel a mix of relief and guilt. Relief because I knew that I was finally safe from his toxic presence, but guilt because I couldn't shake the feeling that somehow, I had contributed to his downward spiral. Mark remained in the hospital, and I began to rebuild my life. It was hard at first but after some time, a little bit of liquor and some help from some friends, I finally did it. It was like stepping out of a dark tunnel into the sunlight. I reconnected with more friends I had lost touch with pursued hobbies that had long been neglected and focused on healing myself from the emotional scars left by our relationship. Rebuilding myself after he left was the best thing that had ever happened to me. I really began to appreciate so many things I took for granted. Unfortunately, this piece wasn't going to last.

I never could have anticipated the terrifying turn my life would take after Mark's release from the mental ward. I had hoped that he would find some semblance of peace or seek help for his own well-being, but instead, he embarked on a path of destruction that almost claimed my life. Apparently, he had become even more consumed by his obsession with me. He convinced his parents that he was in a healthier state of mind and was ready for a fresh start. Believing their son, they released him and helped get him back on his feet.

One fateful day, I had called in sick to work due to some unfriendly and vengeful sushi. A coworker of mine needed the hours and took the shift for me. If you have ever worked retail before you would know that this lady, Rachel, was a unicorn of a woman. Thanks to her I was able to stay home and nurse myself back to health.

However, I was completely unaware of the danger that awaited me had I gone in. Little did I know that Mark had planned to come to my workplace with a gun, fueled by his anger and resentment towards me. He came in and pointed the gun at poor Rachel's head. He kept screaming at her to tell me where I was. Just writing this is making me nauseous. It sends shivers down my spine even now, thinking about what could have happened if I had been there. When yelling at her wasn't enough he started to beat her with the gun. Thankfully, someone near my workplace overheard the chaos and had done something about it. He called the police. The authorities arrived just in time to prevent a tragedy.

Mark was apprehended, and Rachel had some cuts and bruises but overall, she was ok, but I think she will be in therapy for a long time after something like this. When I think back about that one twist of fate- the trauma of that day still haunts me to this day. The realization that my life was so close to being snuffed out by someone I once loved is a heavy burden to bear. Now, Mark sits behind bars, serving time for his actions. It brings some sense of relief knowing that he is no longer a threat to me or anyone else. At least for now. However, the knowledge that he will be eligible for parole in just five years fills me with anxiety and uncertainty.

I find myself at a crossroads once again, unsure of what steps to take next. The scars left by our tumultuous relationship run deep, and I know that healing will take time. But one thing is certain: I refuse to let Mark's presence continue to dictate my life.

I am determined to move forward, to reclaim my sense of safety and rebuild the life that was shattered by his abuse. I will continue seeking therapy and support from loved ones who have stood by me throughout this ordeal. Together, we will navigate the challenges ahead and ensure that I am protected from any further harm.

* * *

STALKED: VOLUME 1

Chapter Six

THE FARMER'S MARKET

As I wandered through the farmers market, my heart weighing heavy with the memories of my recent breakup, I swung my little green hand basket back and forth, trying to shift the currents of my mind. I sought solace among the empty aisles. Always void of humans, the fruit section became my refuge, a sanctuary of vibrant colors and intoxicating aromas. With each step, I inhaled deeply, becoming alive and hoping to lift my spirits with the fragrant offerings before me.

And if all else failed and my spirits never went into orbit again, I could always get a cucumber or two. I suppose I could get a few of the baby ones and pickle them. I mean, after all, it *was* Saturday night and sometimes a girl just needs a good gherkin.

I decided that wasn't the mood I wanted to be in. I

didn't want to rip his tiny little pinhead off any more. You know, I deserve better than him. What's that saying? I thought the five second rule only applied to food I dropped?

What you think about you bring about, and I was bringing a great guy to me. That's what I'm going to manifest. And with that thought, I decided to continue searching the fruit section, searching for the most stimulating items this garden of Eden had to offer. If anything, that would reframe my mind and put me on track to success.

The sweet scent of ripe peaches and the tang of citrus danced in the air, casting a spell of rejuvenation upon my weary soul. My fingers brushed against the velvety skin of a peach, reminding me of nights I spent drawing my finger over his chest, a most gentle hint of life's delicate touch. I looked at the abundance of plump grapes, the hard, juicy watermelons, and succulent apricots. I knew if I stole away in a corner and had a bite, just one bite, the juice would trickle down my chin and follow the curve of my neck and down into my bodice.

And then, I would be sticky with the first bite of summer's bounty. No one wants to walk around sticky. Especially in summer. Let's reel that thought back in, missy.

I knew if I were to never find love in life, at least I

would love myself. And with that thought, I turned to find the best of the farmers market. I deserved the best. I found peace in the promise of new beginnings and the flavors waiting to be savored. The fruit section of the market became my haven, nurturing not only my cravings for freshness but also my spirit, slowly mending the fragments of a broken heart.

I leisurely perused the rows, picking up various pieces of fruit and inhaling their aromas deeply. I closed my eyes and took a deep breath, the fresh smell of a basket of strawberries. I smiled, and as I slowly opened my eyes there before me, on the other side of the display, stood the man of my dreams. It was if the gods read my mind and fashioned him from the display of plantains that lay before him.

He exuded an air of confidence that was impossible to ignore. With each step, he effortlessly commanded attention. His well-fitted attire accentuated his athletic build, while his tousled hair hinted at a touch of ruggedness. Time seemed to slow as our paths momentarily intersected, and our eyes briefly connected, sparking a subtle yet undeniable sense of intrigue. In that fleeting moment the surrounding bustle of the store muted. Only he and I existed on this earth and I became alive again. The possibility of an unexpected encounter hung tantalizingly in the air, leaving me eager to explore the potential hidden within the aisles of the market.

I began channeling my inner Marylin. With a breathy whisper I leaned forward and asked him, "do you like these melons?". His eyes popped open as he looked up, not believing what he just heard.

I, of course, was talking about the cantaloupe, which was on sale, two for three dollars.

As our eyes met, I smiled delicately, batting my lashes like a foolish Southern girl on a first date in the 1950s. Little did he know, I was the reigning queen of double entendre, three years running.

He was trying to stifle a blush and told me the melons looked nice, very firm. I had no comeback, so I nodded and smiled. I picked up two melons, weighing them carefully in each hand, trying to determine which was the heaviest. I'm not sure why I did that, they were on sale and I needed two anyway. I placed them in my little green basket and smiled at him as I turned to walk further down the aisle. Swinging my basket like I was little red riding hood on the way to grandma's, I took a few steps forward. I could hear him step in sync with me. I took two more steps, in order to test my theory. He followed, in pursuit.

I stopped short, reaching back to squeeze a tomato. He didn't realize I had stopped and he ran into me, pressing his vegetable selections into the small of my back. He quickly apologized and as I turned to face him my eyes inadvertently met his. The world was now completely gone, leaving only the two of us in that electrifying moment. Our gazes locked, and an ineffable connection coursed through me like a bolt of lightning. Our eyes spoke volumes, sharing unspoken stories and whispered promises. In that instant, life melted away, and it was just he and I, bathed in a soft, ethereal glow.

Our souls recognized one another, intertwining in a dance of destiny that transcended the boundaries of time and space. It was in that sacred instant that I knew, without a doubt, that this chance encounter would forever alter the course of my life, filling my heart with a love that defied all odds. The symphony of our connection echoed within me, leaving an indelible mark on my soul, forever etching his presence into the tapestry of my life.

Standing in the berry section, our bodies now pressed against each other, he asked if I was always this fun. I told him, "Only in the fruit section. Take me over to the meat case and it's a whole 'nuther story".

With each breath shared and each heartbeat that echoed in sync, the magnetic pull between us grew stronger, intensifying our desire. The mere brush of his fingertips against my skin sent shivers down my spine, awakening a hunger that burned deep within my core. Our encounter became a sensuous exploration, as we unveiled each other's hidden desires, exploring the depths of pleasure with an insatiable hunger. Trying to pull myself away and regaining any semblance of sanity, I joked about things like this never happened when you get curbside pickup..

As the days unfolded, our paths continued to intertwine, magnetically drawing us closer. Each encounter, whether planned or serendipitous, ignited a fire within us that burned with an intensity impossible to ignore. Our conversations became a delicate dance of innuendos and subtle seduction, a symphony of whispered desires that fueled our passion. The stolen glances and lingering touches only added to the mounting tension between us, heightening the anticipation with each passing moment. We reveled in the thrill of the forbidden, savoring the stolen kisses and clandestine rendezvous that punctuated our shared journey. Our bodies, attuned to the same rhythm, yearned to merge, to become entangled in a fervent embrace that transcended the physical realm.

Stolen moments in secret places unleashed a raw and primal side, where inhibitions melted away and vulnerability became our greatest strength. In his arms, I found sanctuary, a place where time ceased to exist, and we became lost in a passionate dance of laced bodies and unspoken promises. We surrendered ourselves to the intoxicating rhythm of our connection, consumed by a flame that could never be extinguished.

I received a text later the next day, asking if we could meet at the base of the hill, just below the stage that held the summer concerts in town. Ten PM, don't be late. Of course, I said yes. I knew by that time the heat of the sun had dissipated, but the warmth of summer would still wrap her arms around us. I couldn't wait until our covert adventure.

I waited near the rail, overlooking the small pond at the bottom of the hill. He walked up behind me, softly pulling my hair to one side and began to kiss my neck. I couldn't resist but I had to tell him - sorry, I was waiting for someone. He laughed quietly and nibbled on my neck and pulled me in, closer to his body. He told me he had a surprise for me and to close my eyes. Carefully he spun me around and there, beneath the oak tree, was my surprise.

Under the starlit sky, we embraced, our souls drawn in to the magic of a midnight picnic. The moon, a silent witness to our whispered vows, cast a soft glow upon the secluded spot we had discovered. A blanket spread out on the lush grass, adorned with flickering candles and a basket filled with delectable treats, set the stage for a night of enchantment. The gentle breeze carried with it the scent of wildflowers, mingling with the melodies of nature, creating a symphony of serenity. As we sat side by side, our fingertips delicately intertwined, time seemed to suspend, allowing us to bask in the magic of the moment.

In the midst of laughter and heartfelt conversations, a crescendo of emotions swelled within us, until we could no longer deny the powerful magnetism pulling us together. With a single touch, the floodgates of desire opened, and we succumbed to the irresistible force that had bound us. In a delicate ballet of passion and tenderness, we shared stolen kisses that stirred a kaleidoscope of emotions within our souls. Wrapped in each other's arms, our hearts beat in unison, creating a rhythm that echoed through the universe. In that intoxicating embrace, we whispered promises of love and devotion, knowing that this extraordinary night would forever be etched in the tapestry of our shared history.

As we sought comfort in the intimacy of the moment, time seemed to stand still. Like two teenagers lost in the throes of young love and nestled in the back of a station wagon, our lips met in a symphony of soft, lingering kisses, each touch igniting a fire within our souls. Hours slipped away unnoticed as we explored the depths of our connection, savoring the sweetness that danced upon our lips.

The world around us no longer exited. With each kiss, a surge of electric passion coursed through our veins, sending shivers of anticipation down our spines. In the dimly lit space, the air was filled with the intoxicating scent of love and vulnerability. Like two souls intertwined, we reveled in the purity of the moment, cherishing each tender caress and breathless sigh that whispered of a love so profound.

Beneath a canopy of stars, we were transported off planet, to a universe where time and responsibility ceased to exist. It was a stolen paradise, a sanctuary of forgotten youth and unadulterated affection. With each kiss, we rediscovered the innocence and intensity of first love.

In the stillness of that serene evening, as the moon cast its gentle glow upon us, we found the courage to bare our souls and profess our love. Words flowed freely from our lips, carrying the weight of a lifetime's worth of emotions. With unwavering sincerity, we laid bare the depths of our hearts, expressing a love that surpassed anything we had ever experienced before. In that vulnerable moment, we both realized that what we shared was extraordinary, a connection that defied all expectations and limitations.

As we spoke, it became clear that this love we had discovered was unlike anything either of us had ever known. It was a love that breathed life into our very beings, infusing each day with an unparalleled excitement and joy. Our hearts beat in unison, harmonizing with a rhythm that echoed throughout our shared existence. We marveled at the way our souls seemed to recognize each other, as if we were kindred spirits brought together by fate itself. In that declaration of love, we found peace and vali-dation, knowing that what we had discovered was a rare gem, a once-in-a-lifetime connection that would forever shape our lives.

He gazed at me with eyes filled with an honest and pure love. I felt a rush of emotions overwhelm my senses. It was a look that penetrated deep into my soul, unraveling the layers of my being and exposing my vulnerability. In that moment, the world around us faded into insignificance. My heart, already captivated by his presence, began to race with an intensity I had never experienced before. Each beat reverberated through my chest, resonating with a strength that threatened to break free from the confines of my ribcage.

I was consumed by a whirlwind of emotions, feeling a mixture of exhilaration and vulnerability intertwining within me. The sheer power of his gaze ignited a fire that burned fiercely within my core, igniting a profound longing that had lain dormant for far too long. It was a moment of transcendence, where words became unnecessary, for our hearts spoke a language understood only by us. In the intensity of that gaze, I knew that this love was unlike anything I had ever encountered. It was a love that defied logic, surpassing mere infatuation or desire. It was a love that touched the depths of my being, transforming me, and making me believe in the extraordinary power of true love.

In a hushed tone, he expressed his gratitude for that

fateful day at the farmers market, where our paths intersected and our destinies intertwined. With a sincerity that
resonated in every word, he confessed that meeting me had
become the turning point, the catalyst that breathed new
life into his world. He spoke of the profound impact I had
on his heart and soul, and how the moments we shared
had opened his eyes to a future filled with boundless
excitement and adventure.

As his voice carried the weight of his dreams and aspi-
rations, I couldn't help but be swept away by the
enchanting vision he painted. Together, we would embrace
each sunrise and sunset as a gift, savoring every twist and
turn that life would offer. He spoke of a future where our
souls would dance amidst the unknown, fearlessly
exploring the depths of love and embracing the uncharted
territories of passion. In his words, I glimpsed a profound
commitment, a promise to nurture the flame of our
connection and face the world hand in hand. The sheer
romanticism of his sentiments filled my heart with an overwhelming sense of hope and possibility, as I eagerly
embraced the shared journey that awaited us, forever
grateful for the serendipity that brought us together.

Chapter Seven

LOVES LOST EMBRACE

I met him on a cool autumn evening; the leaves painted the world with shades of gold. It was a chance encounter. His name was Alexander, and his eyes sparkled with a warmth that instantly drew me in. From that moment, I knew I was in love.

We found ourselves in the same coffee shop, seeking refuge from the chilly winds that whispered through the city streets. As I sipped my coffee, our eyes met across the crowded room. There was an instant connection, an invisible thread that tied us together. With a hesitant smile, he approached, his voice carrying a hint of intrigue.

"Mind if I join you?" he asked, his voice as smooth as Ghirardelli chocolate.

I gestured to the empty seat across from me, unable to

hide my excitement. "Please, be my guest." And so, we spent that evening lost in conversation, our words flowing effortlessly like a gentle river. We talked about our dreams, our passions, and the little intricacies of life that often go unnoticed. It felt as though we had known each other for a lifetime.

Alexander possessed a quiet strength, a pillar of support that grounded me when life seemed uncertain. He quickly became my anchor, the steady heartbeat that echoed in my soul. In his arms, I found a sanctuary from the chaos of the world. Our love was a refuge, a haven where we could be our truest selves.

The crisp autumn air whispered promises of adventure as Alexander and I decided to embark on a spontaneous getaway. With a longing for tranquility and the vibrant colors of the changing leaves, we set our sights on Vermont, a picturesque haven nestled amidst nature's embrace. The open road stretched before us, an invitation to explore the unknown. Taking the top down, we drove through winding country lanes, laughter filled the air, punctuated by the soft melody of our favorite songs. With each passing mile, our spirits soared, and my love for him deepened.

In the heart of the picturesque countryside, we stumbled upon a charming bed and breakfast, a hidden gem exuding warmth and serenity. The moment we stepped through the door, we were greeted with a warmth I had never felt before. The innkeeper, a kind-hearted woman named Margaret, welcomed us as if we were old friends, sharing stories of the area's rich history and guiding us to our cozy suite. The room, adorned with quaint antique furniture and a crackling fireplace, instantly felt like home.

As the moon cast a gentle glow upon the landscape, Alexander and I found ourselves lost in each other's arms. Our connection deepened, a dance of souls harmonizing with the symphony of the night. Time stood still as we whispered sweet nothings, tracing the lines of our love story with gentle fingertips. The flames in the fireplace mirrored the passion that burned within us, casting shadows on the walls as our bodies entwined in a tender embrace.

The fire cast a warm light upon the room and created an intimate ambiance that embraced every corner. Alexander and I stood in front of the stone fireplace, the heat of the flames mirrored the rising heat within our souls. In that moment, our eyes locked with a passionate gaze that spoke volumes. With a tender touch, his hand caressed my cheek, and our lips met in a kiss that ignited a firestorm of delight.

The night unfolded like a symphony of desire and

devotion. Each touch, each kiss, was an expression of the love that bound us together. The bed, dressed with soft, inviting sheets, became a canvas for our passion. We explored the depths of intimacy, surrendering to the enchantment that surrounded us. We discovered a profound connection that transcended the physical, leaving us on the etherial plane.

The taste of his lips was both familiar and intoxicating, like the finest wine I had ever savored. It was a kiss that hinted of promises unspoken, of a love that transcended mere words. Our bodies gravitated towards one another, an undeniable magic brought us closer. The world around us ceased to exist. We melted into each other's embrace, our hearts beating in perfect synchrony.

The heat of the fire embraced us, we found ourselves irresistibly drawn to the bed, an oasis of softness and temptation. It beckoned to us, whispering promises of shared pleasures and blissful surrender. The crisp linens enticed us to sink into their embrace, to lose ourselves in a dance of passion and vulnerability. We succumbed to the alluring call and our bodies forged together with an intensity that left us breathless and hungry for more.

The night unfolded like a symphony of desire and longing. Every touch, every caress, fueled the flames of our insatiable hunger for one another. We reveled in the exploration of each other's bodies, navigating the contours and valleys of our love with reverence and adoration. The room echoed with our shared moans and sighs, a soundtrack to our journey into the realms of ecstasy.

Moving in harmony, our bodies became a dance of love and fulfillment. With each whispered word, with every stroke of our fingertips, we unraveled the depths of passion and intimacy. Time became fluid, merging with the rhythm of our bodies, as we surrendered ourselves to the intoxicating symphony of pleasure.

As the night waned and the first rays of dawn caressed the room, we lay in each other's arms, breathless and satiated. Our bodies and souls had danced a dance of unadulterated passion, leaving an indelible imprint upon our hearts. We basked in the afterglow, our souls intertwined, knowing that this night of unforgettable intimacy had bound us together in a way that could never be undone.

In the stillness of that moment, I whispered words of love and gratitude to Alexander, the man who had unlocked the deepest recesses of my heart. We drifted into a peaceful slumber, our bodies and spirits entangled, I knew that this night of transcendent passion would forever be etched in the annals of our love story.

The first rays of sunlight filtered through the curtains, casting a soft glow upon the room as Alexander stirred awake. His eyes, still heavy with sleep, met mine, and a tender smile graced his lips. As he rose from the bed, his presence filled the room with an air of warmth and contentment. Stretching his arms above his head, he leaned down to press a gentle kiss on my forehead, promising to return soon with the elixir of life we called coffee.

With a murmured "I'll be right back, my love," Alexander made his way towards the door. I watched him, a mixture of affection and anticipation, as he moved with the grace of a man who knew he held my heart in the palm of his hand. I heard the sound of the jeep starting, accompanied by the familiar crunch of gravel beneath the tires. I listened intently as the vehicle slowly backed out of the drive, carrying Alexander away, leaving me with the bittersweet ache of longing for his return.

I knew this was my chance for a long, hot shower. I stepped into the steam-filled tub, the hot water cascading over my weary body. Each droplet was a gentle caress, washing away any anguish and sorrow that ever clung to my soul. As the warmth wrapped around me, my aching muscles began to relax, and a sense of renewal washed over me like a gentle wave. The steam mingled with my tears of happiness. I let them flow freely, a release from the grief and longing I had clung on to for my entire life. In that solitary moment, the water became a balm for my wounded heart, soothing the ache that seemed unbearable. I knew then, I was finally free from my past.

Stepping out of the revitalizing shower, I wrapped myself in a plush towel, the comforting warmth soothing my chilled skin. Expecting to find Alexander waiting for me with a smile and a hot steaming cup of coffee, my heart sank as I realized he hadn't returned yet. Frowning, I slipped into my clothes, a mix of anticipation and concern swirling within me.

Determined to make the most of the day, I began planning our itinerary, envisioning the adventures we would embark on together. But as minutes turned into hours, a gnawing unease settled in the pit of my stomach. It was unlike Alexander to be gone for so long without a word. My mind spun with worry, conjuring up countless scenarios, each one more harrowing than the last.

Time stretched on, and the weight of uncertainty grew heavier with each passing moment. Anxiety wrapped its talons around me, constricting my chest and clouding my thoughts. Where could he be? Doubts and fears whispered in my ear, threatening to suffocate the flame of hope. In the depths of my worry, I knew I had to take action, to find answers and bring peace to my restless heart.

A heaviness settled within me as I made the decision to descend the staircase, my footsteps slow and deliberate. But as I reached the halfway point, a sight froze me in place. Margaret, the innkeeper, stood at the foot of the stairs, her shoulders trembling, flanked by two solemn police officers. Tears streamed down her face, her grief evident, and in that instant, a horrifying realization pierced through me like a jagged blade. Something terrible had happened.

Horror coursed through my veins as I took in the scene before me, the weight of tragedy crushing my spirit. Margaret's watery eyes met mine, filled with an anguish that words could never express. She opened her trembling lips, her voice choked with sorrow, and in a pained whisper, she uttered those words I feared most: "Oh, my dear. I'm so sorry."

I was in a vacuum. The air was ripped from my lungs, pulling the last remaining drops of blood from my shattered heart. The room spun around me, and I clung to the banister for support, feeling as though the ground beneath me had given way. In that moment, a profound grief washed over me, overwhelming my senses.

"No. Nooo. Nooooooooo." I collapsed to the stairs, my dreams and my life falling down around me.

Like sand through my fingers, a year passed away. The world had moved on while I remained trapped in the clutches of my grief. I walked the familiar streets of my neighborhood, each step heavy with the weight of love lost. The once vibrant surroundings had turned into a haze of muted colors, reflecting the numbness that had settled deep within my soul.

The pain of losing Alexander lingered, an ache that refused to subside. I mourned not only the man I had loved so fiercely but also the dreams we had woven together, now scattered like his ashes in the wind. The thought of opening my heart to another seemed unfathomable; the wounds were still raw. The strength that had once propelled me forward had dissipated, leaving behind a hollow emptiness.

As I sat down on a weathered park bench, a heavy sigh escaped my lips, carrying with it the weight of my sorrow. Even nature sensed my desolation. Squirrels scurried closer, their playful antics and chattering serving as a gentle distraction from my pain. Birds chirped overhead, their songs a soothing salve to my wounded heart. It was in these simple moments of solace that I found a glimmer of solace, a reminder that life continued to unfold despite my own despair.

Lost in my thoughts, I glanced up, and for a fleeting moment, my heart leaped within my chest. In the distance, amidst the dappled sunlight, I thought I caught a glimpse of a familiar form. It was Alexander - or at least, it seemed like him. My breath hitched, hope rekindling within me like a dormant flame. Time seemed to freeze as my gaze locked onto his figure, his features a blur in the distance.

But as quickly as hope had emerged, it was extinguished. Like a wisp of smoke, Alexander vanished, leaving behind an emptiness that gnawed at my soul. Doubt crept in and I questioned if my eyes had played tricks on me.

I began to wonder: did love have the power to survive even beyond death? It was a notion that simultaneously terrified and fascinated me. If love could transcend the boundaries of mortality, then perhaps there was hope for the shattered pieces of my soul.

Driven by an insatiable curiosity, I returned to the park the next day. As I settled onto the same bench, a mixture of trepidation and yearning coursed through my veins. The universe had conspired to grant my deepest wish, there he was again, Alexander, his presence shimmering before me like a mirage.

In an attempt to run to him I jumped from the bench. As my feet touched the ground, the ethereal apparition before me vanished, leaving behind an empty space that echoed my shattered hopes. The realization washed over me. The love we shared had transcended the realm of the living, existing only as a poignant memory.

I rushed home, my heart pounding in my chest. Thoughts whirled in my mind, a flurry of hopes, doubts, and unspoken desires. The weight of what I had witnessed in the park lingered, fueling a sense of determination that bordered on desperation. I needed to reach out to Alexander, to bridge the gap between our worlds.

In the solitude of my home, I whispered his name. I closed my eyes, envisioning him standing before me, his eyes filled with warmth and understanding. I willed him to return to me, to manifest in a way that my senses could perceive. I pleaded with the universe, the very essence of my plea echoed in the chambers of my soul.

And in the hushed moments that followed, a stillness settled over me. The universe, too, held its breath, waiting for a response. The room remained empty; a silence hung heavy in the air. Tears welled up in my eyes, a mixture of frustration and aching longing. I realized that no matter how fiercely I desired his return, the power to bridge the gap between our worlds eluded me. I was left with the bittersweet realization that love, even in its most profound form, couldn't always defy the boundaries of existence.

Days drifted by, each one blending into the next as I went about the routines of life. On a seemingly ordinary afternoon, I stood at the sink, absentmindedly washing my lunch dishes as my mind wandered to memories of Alexander. Lost in reverie, I looked up and caught sight of movement in the window's reflection. My heart leaped with an inexplicable hope as I turned. A plate slipped from my hand and crashed to the floor. But as my eyes scanned the room, searching for the source of the reflection, I was met only with an empty space, devoid of any physical presence.

Tears welled up in my eyes, mingling with the fragments of broken porcelain at my feet. The ache within me deepened, a mixture of longing and resignation. The ethereal connection that had once bound us seemed to have grown faint, teasing me with glimpses and whispers, only to withdraw in the next breath. And yet, despite the disappointment, a flicker of hope remained, a quiet belief that the bond we shared, though elusive, persisted in the intangible realms that lay beyond the world of the living.

Overwhelmed by the swirling emotions and the unexplainable glimpses of Alexander's presence, I reached out to my dear friend Holly, hoping she could provide some clarity in the midst of my confusion. With a trembling voice, I shared my fears of losing my sanity, of teetering on the precipice of a reality I couldn't comprehend.

To my relief, Holly assured me she had an answer, a glimmer of understanding that could potentially shed light on the enigmatic occurrences. The following day, we went to a small, dimly lit room where a psychic awaited, her eyes shimmering with a wisdom that seemed to span beyond the confines of mortal knowledge.

I sat before the psychic, her gaze seemed to penetrate deep into the depths of my soul. With a gentle touch, she took my trembling hands and spoke words that both soothed and unsettled my troubled heart. She explained that Alexander's spirit remained bound to this earthly plane, tethered by the intensity of our love and my unwavering longing. His essence lingered, trapped in the ether, unable to fully move forward.

Her voice quivered with a mix of empathy and conviction as she encouraged me to release him, to let go of the hold I unknowingly exerted. It was a profound revelation, a truth that resonated deep within me. As difficult as it was to fathom, I understood that by clinging to him, I had inadvertently kept him from his own journey of transcendence.

The psychic's words offered a glimmer of hope amid the anguish. She assured me that our souls were destined to reunite, that the divine tapestry had woven our paths together for a reason. Alexander was not lost forever; he was simply caught in the delicate balance of reality. In the depths of my heart, I vowed to find the strength to release him, to honor our love by allowing him the freedom to embrace his destiny, trusting that our reunion would come when the time was right.

That night, I adorned our room with candles, their warm glow casting shadows upon the walls. The soft, golden light filled the room, creating an ethereal ambiance that mirrored the tumultuous emotions within me. I sat upon our bed and called to Alexander. I closed my eyes and allowed my imagination to paint a vivid picture of him standing before me, his presence palpable.

In the depths of my mind's eye, I could see his figure, his features bathed in a soft radiance. I reached out, longing to feel the warmth of his touch, the strength of his embrace. In that sacred space between reality and dreams, our spirits touched once more. With tender intensity, we shared one last kiss, a bittersweet fusion of love and farewell.

His hand gently cupped my cheek, his touch both tender and fleeting. A smile graced his lips, a silent reassurance that lingered in the air, and then, with a whisper, he vanished like a wisp of smoke. In that moment, a mixture of sorrow and peace washed over me. I knew that this farewell was not an end but a beginning. It was a poignant transition, a letting go that allowed both of our souls to embark on the journeys that awaited us.

As the candles continued to cast their gentle glow, I lay there in the stillness of the night, knowing our love would endure, transcending the boundaries of time and space. Alexander, my divine partner, would forever hold a place in my heart, and one day when our souls once again converged, we would find love again in each other's embrace. Until that day arrived, I carried his essence within me, a beacon of love guiding me through the vast expanse of my own journey. I understood that love, in its purest form, defied the boundaries of mortality. It was a force that endured, even when the physical presence was gone. And though I longed for his touch, his voice, his warm embrace, I took comfort knowing the love we had shared would forever be a part of me, guiding me through the darkest of nights and lighting my path towards a future where love and loss coexisted.

Chapter Eight

THE BOTTLE

As I walked along the sandy shores of the beach in North Carolina, the salty breeze kissed my face, carrying with it the whispers of the sea. It was a serene evening. The sun slowly setting and casted a golden hue over the endless expanse of water. Lost in my thoughts, I found tranquility in the rhythmic sound of crashing waves, seeking refuge from the chaos of my own life. The beach was my sanctuary, a place where I could escape and find peace in the embrace of nature.

I had always been drawn to the ocean, finding comfort in its vastness and the way it mirrored the complexities of life. Growing up in a small coastal town, the beach held a special place in my heart. It was where I had spent countless summer days with my family, building sandcastles and chasing seagulls. The dunes later provided places to escape with friends and remain hidden from the world. The bonfires at night drew us all together and bonds, stronger than the ties of a sail, were forged. As time passed, life took its toll, scattering us to different corners of the world.

Now, here I was, walking alone, retracing the steps of my childhood and longing for the simplicity of those care-free days.

The gentle lapping of the waves seemed to invite me further down the shoreline, enticing me to explore the mysteries that lay hidden in the sand. As I continued my stroll, I couldn't help but wonder what stories the ocean held. I continued to walk along the sandy beach and a glint of green glass caught my eye, partially concealed by the soft grains of sand. My curiosity piqued, I reached down and gently tugged at the mysterious object. To my surprise, I unearthed an old bottle, weathered and worn from its time at sea. Fate had guided me to this spot, presenting me with a hidden treasure waiting to be discovered.

With trembling hands, I carefully extracted the tightly rolled pieces of paper from within the bottle's neck. The once-white parchment had yellowed with age, and the edges were frayed and delicate. It bore the signs of count-less journeys, just like the bottle that had brought it to my feet.

Intrigued by its contents, I gingerly unfolded the faded papers, afraid that it might crumble in my hands. The ink, once vibrant and bold, had faded to a mere whisper of its former glory. Words appeared like ethereal whispers, their meaning shrouded in the passage of time. But as I squinted and strained, I could decipher fragments of a heartfelt message, a testament to a love that had stood the test of time. It was a love that transcended the boundaries of distance and defied the odds, a love that yearned to be heard and understood.

In that moment, holding the fragile remnants of some-one's intimate thoughts, I felt an inexplicable connection. The spirits of the sea had chosen me to be the custodian of this extraordinary love story. With a mix of reverence and anticipation, I vowed to piece together the puzzle, to breathe life back into the faded words, and to honor the lovers who had shared their hearts through the art of written expression.

I unfolded the weathered letter, the words danced before my eyes, revealing a tale that ignited my imagina-tion. The author, a woman named Isabella, poured her heart onto the pages, infusing every word with a potent mix of passion, longing, and regret. Through her eloquent prose, I glimpsed into the extraordinary love story that had unfolded in her life.

Isabella's words spoke of a fateful encounter on a stormy night, when she crossed paths with a captivating man named Gabriel. Their connection was instantaneous, as if destiny had woven their lives together. From that moment on, they embarked on a whirlwind romance that spanned continents and defied all odds. The intensity of their love was palpable, seeping through each line Isabella penned, drawing me further into their enchanting world.

From the first line of Isabella's letter, I was captivated. I wanted to know more about her incredible life. Intrigued by the hidden treasure I had discovered, I decided to venture further down the beach, hoping to uncover more bottles and fragments of Isabella and Gabriel's love story. The salty air draped around me, carrying with it the secrets of the sea, urging me onward.

As I wandered along the shoreline, my eyes keenly scanned the sandy landscape, searching for any signs of hidden treasures waiting to be found. And there, nestled under the edge of the dunes, I spotted three more bottles, half-buried and concealed from the casual observer. A thrill coursed through me as I crouched down, eagerly reaching for the first one. With a gentle tug, I pulled it free from its sandy embrace, my heart racing in anticipation. The second and third bottles followed suit, each one revealing its own faded message, fragments of Isabella's heartfelt letters.

As I sat down by the water's edge, I carefully unfolded the pages, one by one, studying the delicate script that told the tale of Isabella and Gabriel's extraordinary love. With reverence, I read Isabella's words, feeling the depth of her emotions seep into my own soul. The letters painted a portrait of a love so profound, so encompassing, that it defied the boundaries of time and distance.

With each page, the pieces of their story began to intertwine, like the brushstrokes of a masterful painting. I could sense the ebb and flow of their relationship, the moments of blissful togetherness and the pangs of longing when they were apart. I read about their adventures, their shared dreams, and the promises they made to one another.

As I pieced together the fragments of Isabella's letters, a clearer picture of their love story emerged. Their love was a tapestry woven with threads of passion, resilience, and unwavering devotion. I marveled at the strength of their connection, despite the challenges they faced. Their story spoke of the power of love transcending barriers, to bridge the gaps between two souls yearning to be together.

Lost in her words, I became a guardian of their story, a custodian of their love. With each letter, my heart swelled with empathy for Isabella and Gabriel, their experiences etching themselves into my very being. I had always dreamed that such love was real, that lives like this were actually lived. The bottles began to fill me with the elixir of hope, and I thought that perhaps that someday, I would find a love like this. As I gazed out at the endless expanse of the sea, I wiped the tears from my eyes. I felt a profound sense of gratitude for having been chosen to bear witness to their tale, to ensure that their love story would not be forgotten.

The path of their love, however, was not without obstacles. Gabriel, a talented artist with a restless spirit, often found himself torn between his insatiable wander-lust and the profound love he felt for Isabella. As I read Isabella's heartfelt words, I could sense her struggle, torn between the desire to hold on and the fear of losing Gabriel to the call of adventure.

Their love story was a tango of joy and pain, filled with stolen moments and passionate embraces. They reveled in each other's company, cherishing the rare instances when their paths converged. But as their connection deepened, so did the weight of their circumstances.

Isabella's words carried a sense of yearning, almost of a hope that was lost. Yet, beneath the surface of their love story, there lay a bittersweet undercurrent of regret. Isabella hinted at missed opportunities and choices that had shaped their lives. She spoke of sacrifices made in the name of love, and the scars that adorned their souls as a result. It was a reminder that even the most extraordinary love stories are not immune to the complexities and hard-ships that life often throws in our path.

As I immersed myself in the pages of Isabella's letters,

the world in which she and Gabriel lived came alive before my eyes. They were not just two lovers, but inhabitants of Paris at the turn of the century, a city teeming with art, culture, and endless possibilities. Through Isabella's eloquent words, I glimpsed the vibrant streets of Montmartre, the whispers of music from the grand salons, and the bustling cafés that fueled their passions.

But their idyllic life was not without its share of heartbreak. In one of Isabella's pages, she revealed the devastating loss they had endured - a young daughter - taken too soon by a cruel twist of fate. The weight of that tragedy cast a shadow over their lives, stealing away the light that once danced in Isabella's eyes. I could feel her grief, her longing for a child she would never hold again, a pain that reverberated through her words and etched itself onto the yellowed pages.

In the midst of their sorrow, World War I loomed on the horizon, threatening to shatter the fragile peace they had managed to carve out for themselves. Gabriel, ever the protector, insisted on leaving Paris, sensing the impending storm that would sweep through their beloved city. With great difficulty they escaped, leaving behind the place that had witnessed their love's blossoming and their shared dreams taking flight.

As I read about their escape, I couldn't help but imagine the heart-wrenching decisions they had to make, the torn loyalties and the overwhelming fear that clung to their every step. Through Isabella's letters, I felt the tension in the air, the palpable uncertainty that weighed heavily on their shoulders. It was a testament to their resilience, their determination to keep their love alive amidst the chaos and turmoil of war.

Isabella's words conveyed the pain and longing of a woman torn between her love for Gabriel and her yearning for the life they had left behind. In the midst of the world descending into madness, they clung to their love as an anchor, a lifeline that gave them hope amidst the darkness. Their story was one of courage, of navigating through treacherous waters and emerging on the other side, forever changed but still fiercely connected.

As I closed the final letter, the echoes of Isabella and Gabriel's love resonated within me. Their story transcended time and space, their struggles and triumphs etching themselves upon my heart. I found myself wanting more of their story, but there were no more bottles to be found. I scoured the beach for weeks, all summer, but no other bottle surfaced. I was doomed to never knowing how their love story ended.

With a few weeks of summer still lingering in the air, the anticipation of the end-of-summer bonfire grew within me. It was a tradition that brought old friends together, a chance to bask in the warmth of nostalgia and create new memories. As the day drew nearer, I couldn't help but feel a mix of excitement and trepidation. So much had changed since the last time we gathered; I wondered if I would still fit into the familiar group dynamics.

The truth was, I didn't feel like the same person I used to be. Life had thrown its curveballs, leaving me with scars and lessons that had shaped my perspective. I had grown, evolved, and embarked on a journey of self-discovery. I had shed an old skin and emerged anew, with a sense of purpose and a hunger for authenticity. But with this transformation came the fear that I had outgrown my place among my childhood friends.

As the bonfire night approached, I couldn't help but wrestle with the insecurities that gnawed at me. Would they still see me as the person they once knew? Would I be able to bridge the gap between who I used to be and who I had become? The fear of not fitting in lingered in my mind, casting shadows on the excitement that should have been all-consuming. Yet, deep down, I knew that true friends would see beyond the surface and embrace the growth and change within me. They would understand that life had sculpted me into someone different, someone stronger. And so, with a mixture of hope and apprehension, I prepared to go to the bonfire, ready to reunite with my old companions and discover if our connections could withstand the transformation. Would we be able to stand up to time like Isabella and Gabriel?.

As I arrived at the bonfire, the crackling flames dancing in the night, I felt a swirl of emotions. Faces familiar yet slightly altered greeted me with warm embraces, their laughter and chatter filling the air. In that moment, I realized that friendships, like love, had the power to withstand the passage of time. We might have grown and changed individually, but the bonds we had forged in our youth remained steadfast.

And so, surrounded by the glow of the fire and the laughter of old friends, I let go of my fears. I discovered that the essence of who I had become only added depth and richness to our connections. It was a reminder that true friendships had the capacity to evolve alongside us, embracing the changes and celebrating the growth. In that night of reunion, I found solace in the warmth of their acceptance, and I knew that I had never truly lost my place among them.

The last embers of the bonfire dwindled as I said my goodbyes to old friends. After our arms released the last of our hugs, I turned to walk down the beach, savoring the final moments of that summer night.

The waves crashed against the shore, their rhythmic melody soothing my restless mind. Lost in my thoughts, I caught a glimpse of something familiar in the surf, shimmering in the moonlight. A surge of curiosity propelled me forward, my steps quickening as I ran toward the mysterious object.

As I reached the water's edge, I stooped down and plucked the object from the foamy kiss of the waves. It was another green bottle, weathered and worn, a relic from the depths of the sea. A thrill shot through me as I realized it was one last message from Isabella, a final piece to complete the puzzle of their love story. The universe had brought us together one more time, granting me the privilege of unearthing their tale once again.

With trembling hands, I delicately extracted the tightly rolled message from within the bottle. The familiar faded parchment unfurled before my eyes, revealing Isabella's elegant script. It was as if she had whispered across time and space, her words reaching out to touch my heart once more. In that moment, I felt an indescribable connection, a sense of awe that transcended the limitations of the physical world.

Isabella's final letter bore a bittersweet tone, a farewell etched into her words. She expressed gratitude for the memories they had shared, for the love that had enriched their lives, and for the moments they had treasured together. It was a touching reminder that life's seasons are fleeting, and even the most extraordinary love stories must eventually come to an end.

As I read the final faded words of Isabella's letter, I felt a mixture of awe and sadness. Their love had burned bright, its intensity etched into their souls. But fate had dealt them a cruel hand, as I discovered in the final letter that began with the despair of Isabella as she began to chronicle the tragic sinking of their boat. The heartbreaking reality washed over me, tears welling in my eyes as I mourned the loss of their love, forever frozen in time at the bottom of the sea.

As I clutched the last remnants of their life, tears welled in my eyes. Isabella and Gabriel had become more than just characters in a story; they had become a part of my own journey, teaching me about the resilience of the human spirit and the power of enduring love. With a heavy heart, I returned the message to its bottle, releasing it back into the sea, knowing that their story would forever be carried by the waves, a timeless testament to the beauty and fragility of love.

I turned to walk down the beach and the weight of their story settled within me, mingling with the salt-kissed breeze. In that moment, I vowed to carry their memory in my heart, to honor their love by living fully and embracing the fleeting moments that life bestowed upon me. And so, beneath the stars that stretched across the vast expanse of the night sky, I walked into the future, forever touched by the extraordinary love of Isabella and Gabriel.

Chapter Nine

TEMPEST'S EMBRACE

The wind howled outside my window, a constant reminder of the path my life had taken. I found serenity in the chaos and beauty of nature's fury. Raging winds and swirling clouds mirrored the turmoil within me, a microburst of memories and regrets.

One of my first memories is of a tornado. With little warning, it tore through my town in the middle of the night, taking everything I loved. That memory has always haunted me, shaping me. The dance with danger and the opportunity to capture the breathtaking magnificence of tornadoes became my lifeline. In their presence, I could momentarily forget all the pain that haunted my dreams and embrace a world where the only thing that mattered was the chase.

There was an unbridled passion in storms. The love of dangerous weather raged through my soul like the brightest lightning bolt. I was captivated by the dance between earth and sky, the collision of warm and cold air, the mesmerizing dance of clouds spiraling into a furious funnel. The pursuit of tornadoes became my obsession, my purpose. No one could understand my passion, my unyielding desire to stand in the eye of the storm. But for me, it was a chance to face my demons head-on. Face the monsters that ripped my life apart. It was my chance to be the victor against death. In those moments, when I stood on the edge of danger, I felt alive. Following tornadoes held the key to unlocking the hidden depths of my soul, allowing me to confront my past and finally find redemption amidst my tears.

I looked to the skies and saw clouds forming a sheer and I knew what that meant. There was a super cell forming and I needed to be at the birth. Quickly I packed my equipment and ran towards my SUV. Rain was beginning and I raced down the drive, heading towards my destiny.

The storm raged with unyielding force and I spotted a figure seeking refuge amidst the storm. There was a car off to the side and in a ditch. I assumed it was his and he did not know how to drive in a "little rain". I pulled off the road, unlocked the door and opened it. "GET IN" I screamed. With rain-soaked hair and eyes gleaming with determination, the wet man possessed an unwavering spirit that mirrored my own. He hopped in and said thanks, then began looking at his phone which revealed an open weather app.

He was able to mutter that his name was Deacon, an ambitious meteorologist. He had always been fascinated by the dance of the elements, driven by a desire to understand and predict the very storms I pursued. He carried with him a deep-seated eagerness to uncover the secrets of the skies, a yearning that matched my own longing for connection and purpose. In his eyes, I saw the reflection of a soul as restless as mine, seeking knowledge and understanding amidst the swirling nature of life's uncertainties. Fate had intertwined our destinies, casting us together in the maelstrom of our shared pursuit.

From the moment I encountered Deacon's dismissive attitude, my temper was instantly set off like lightning in a summer storm. His air of superiority, as if his meteorological knowledge made him the ruler of the skies, grated on my nerves. But beneath my annoyance, there was an undeniable attraction that stirred within me. With his rugged charm and a physique that exuded masculinity, he was the epitome of a hot and manly TV Weather Man.

With the falling barometer, the storm had unleashed a magnetic force between us, drawing us closer with each bolt of lightning. And as fate would have it, the nature of our initial encounter led to unexpected conversations, unveiling hidden depths and shared experiences that forged a connection stronger than I could have imagined. In those moments, our rivalry transformed into something more profound, and I knew that the storm was merely the backdrop to a love story written in the heavens.

As the storm darkened the horizon, its raw power beckoned to both Deacon and me, bridging the divide that had separated us. With a shared determination to face the tornado head-on, we made a pact to team up and chase the storm as one. Our individual strengths and expertise seamlessly mixed, forming an alliance against the raging forces of nature. The dangers that lay ahead only fueled our spirits. We both craved the exhilaration and thrill that came with confronting the untamed elements.

I looked up and saw the clouds had shifted, indicating the leading edge of the cell. "We need to go over there" I said to him. Deacon, ignoring my words, grunted. I took that as a "yes". With his acknowledgement, I slammed on the brakes, tossing him into the dash. "What the hell" he said. I looked at him and told him to hang on and made a slightly illegal U-Turn in the middle of the rain soaked highway, fishtailing at the very end. I looked at him and smiled, batting my eyes and trying to disarm his hostility. "It's only illegal if you get caught" I said, shooting off down the highway and towards the storm.

As the tornado loomed directly before us, threatening to swallow everything in its path, instinct took over, and I knew we had to find shelter to ride out the storm's wrath. I made a decision to veer off the road, seeking refuge in a sturdy shelter. The wind howled as we made a dash for safety. Once inside, I saw the mud caked to my body, my hair gnarled in a matted mess. Deacon was the same, muddy and wet, but safe. I didn't want to be held responsible for the death of the leading local TV Weather Man. I managed to get him to safety, a job well done I thought.

The storm grew in strength and in that confined space, I felt my attraction for him growing stronger, intensifying with every beat of my heart. The air crackled, drawing us closer and created a dance of desire and longing. The squall raged outside, fiercely banging at the door. Inside, we were safe. As far as I was concerned, the world outside disappeared and we were left, just the two of us, in a deluge of emotion.

Within a few moments, the storm shifted again, taking a northerly path. We decided to make a break for it and follow it further. Within moments, the wind began to howl and rain lashed against my SUV, but it was the flashes of lightning and the ominous funnel clouds that truly tested our mettle. The intensity of the storm grew and I saw our bond had begun to solidify. And then, as if the storm itself acknowledged our union, a colossal tornado materialized before us. With hearts pounding, we watched in awe and terror as it crossed directly in front of my SUV, its destructive power a sight to behold. In that moment, we were not just observers; we were part of the storm's dance, feeling its might and majesty reverberate through our very beings.

In the midst of confusion, I could no longer deny the attraction between us. The storm had brought us alive, awakening emotions that had appeared as quickly as the cyclone. I caught Deacon's gaze, and within those stormy depths, I saw a reflection of my own desires mirrored back at me. The whirlwind of nature had swept away the walls I had built, leaving behind an unspoken connection. In that perilous moment, as our lives hung in the balance, I knew that we were not just partners in chasing storms; we were on the leading edge of a love-storm that could withstand anything that Mother Nature threw at us.

The super-storm disappeared as swiftly as it had arrived, leaving behind a sense of calm in its wake. With a collective sigh of relief, Deacon and I decided to venture into the nearby town, looking for someplace where we could shower and clean up from the storm. We were covered in mud and rain and desired to feel human again; only a hot shower could change that. As Deacon stepped out of my SUV, I noticed he looked even more manly-man now. Steam rose from the streets. I thought the steam was from the wet streets heating up, but honestly, at this point I really couldn't be sure.

In our quest for a hot shower, we stumbled upon a quaint hotel tucked away on a quiet street. Its weathered exterior seemed to mirror our own journey, bearing the scars of time and trials. Inside, the lobby exuded a warm and inviting ambiance. It was getting late and we decided to check in for the night, each getting our own rooms. It seemed safer that way. The forecast for the next day called for more of the same and we agreed, we could resume our storm hunting in the morning. However, fate had a whimsical twist in store for us. The hotel had only one available room, a cozy corner suite that seemed to hold the very essence of our intertwined destinies. With a silent understanding passing between us, we made a shared decision to occupy the room together.

As we settled into the room, the air between us hummed with a charge of electricity, the kind you find when low and high pressure cells collide. The room, adorned with rustic charm, felt like a haven from the night.

After the arduous chase and the storm's aftermath, I yearned for the soothing embrace of a hot shower to wash away the remnants of adrenaline and exhaustion. With anticipation coursing through my veins, I stepped under the cascading water, feeling the steam wrap around me like a comforting embrace. The heat penetrated my skin, melting away the tension and leaving me refreshed and renewed. As I emerged from the shower, dressed in an oversized t-shirt that I had hastily stuck away in my SUV, I realized that I was ill-prepared for company.

My damp hair clung to my shoulders as I ventured out of the bathroom, only to find Deacon waiting with an amused smile tugging at the corners of his lips. His gaze briefly flickered over my disheveled appearance, a spark of recognition and desire igniting in his eyes. It was a moment of vulnerability, caught off guard and exposed, but there was an undeniable thrill in his gaze that sent a shiver down my spine. With a playful wink, Deacon wordlessly excused himself, retreating back into the bathroom to indulge in his own well-deserved hot shower. In that fleeting exchange, we both knew that the boundaries we had set for ourselves were beginning to crumble, and a new chapter of our journey was about to unfold.

I settled into the silence of the room; the melodic sound of Deacon's voice reached my ears, mingling with the rhythmic patter of water against porcelain. His captivating voice echoed through the steam-filled bathroom and a harmonious serenade began to wrap around my heart. Moments later, the shower ceased its cascading symphony, and the door swung open, releasing a billowing cloud of steam into the room. From within the mist emerged Deacon, like a god of the storm, his presence commanding attention.

He walked towards me, his muscular body glistening with droplets of water, his bare skin accentuated by the soft towel that clung to his form. The steam seemed to dance around him, teasingly revealing glimpses of his sculpted physique, as if he had stepped out of a dream. With each step, my breath caught in my throat, my pulse quickening as he drew closer. He possessed a magnetic charisma, an aura of confidence that ignited a fire within me. In that moment, I couldn't help but imagine him as the opening act for an all male review, his every movement exuding a sensuality that left me yearning for more. Our eyes locked, and in that smoldering look, I knew that the storm had only just begun.

The soft glow of the bedside lamp cast shadows, dancing across the walls as we hesitated, contemplating the boundaries of our connection. With unspoken words hanging in the air, we came to a silent understanding, an agreement that hinted at a deeper connection that went beyond mere companionship. In that moment, we shed the weight of the past and embraced the unknown, surrendering to the magnetic pull that had brought us together.

The barriers that had once divided us shattered under

the weight of our undeniable attraction. The lines between professional and personal blurred. I watched as Deacon cast away his towel, his chiseled physique still glistening. With an air of confidence, he stepped toward me, his eyes burning with an intensity that set my heart ablaze. In that moment, the world around us faded, leaving only the two of us locked in an electric embrace.

He pulled me close, his strong arms covering me with a warmth that melted my defenses. As our bodies pressed against each other, the world fell away, leaving only the raw and passionate connection between us.

Our lips met, a gentle collision that ignited a thousand storms within me. It was a kiss that spoke of desire and longing, of promises whispered between breaths. In that shared moment, the world disappeared.

The rest of the night was a symphony of passion and discovery. We explored each other's bodies, uncovering the depths of desire that had been suppressed. With each touch, each caress, the flames of our love grew higher, burning away any inhibitions or doubts that may have ever lived.

Underneath the humid sky, we danced to the rhythm of our hearts, losing ourselves in a whirlwind of pleasure and connection. Our bodies moved in perfect harmony, each movement a testament to the bond we shared. The night filled with murmurs of ecstasy, as our souls merged and became one.

Time slipped away unnoticed, hours melting into eternity. We reveled in the beauty of our passion, the enchantment of the night that wrapped us in its embrace. It was a night that would forever be etched in our memories, a night of love and surrender, where we discovered the depths of our hearts and souls.

As the moon glowed brightly through the break in the curtains, we found ourselves entangled in each other's arms, basking in the afterglow of our passion. In that moment, I knew that I had found my forever in Deacon, a love that would endure any storm, any obstacle that life would throw my way. I knew that every moment spent in his arms would be a testament to the power of love and the endless possibilities that awaited us.

The night passed quickly and as I stirred in the morning light, my first instinct was to check Doppler. Squinting at the screen, I saw a cell on the horizon. Nature was preparing to unleash its fury once again.

I shook Deacon, the gravity of the situation etched on my face. We quickly analyzed the radar images, tracing the path of the impending storm front. We calculated its trajectory, the intensity of the storm brewing within us as well.

I knew that we had to act quickly. Gathering our gear,

we ran to my SUV, ready to confront the storm head-on. In that very instant, we were not just storm chasers, but warriors of the elements, ready to face whatever challenges lay in our path. The storm beckoned and we answered its call, knowing that within the chaos, we would find the ecstasy that transcended the power of the storm.

Standing outside the hotel, I saw it in the distance forming on the horizon. Dark clouds swirled, colliding with one another, creating a tango of power and mayhem. I was mesmerized. This was no ordinary storm; it was a force of nature. It was the finger of God, an F5 tornado in the making.

The wind began to pick up, carrying the scent of rain and adventure. My heart raced in sync with the gathering storm. I couldn't tear my eyes away from the display of nature's fury. The storm was calling to me, begging me to chase it.

Deacon's eyes filled with concern. He knew the risks involved, the dangers that awaited if we dared to venture into the heart of the storm. He pleaded with me, begging me to reconsider. His love and concern were palpable, but a part of me craved the thrill of the unknown. I understood Deacon's fears, but I knew this was my calling. It was in those moments, where fear and excitement swirled, I felt the most alive. The storm was a seductive mistress and she was calling to me.

I stood there, the wind tousling my hair. I turned to Deacon and took his hand, squeezing it gently. "I need to go," I whispered, my voice filled with both conviction and vulnerability. "I need to understand." I was ready to face the winds and the unknown. It was a choice fueled by passion, love, and knowing you were tossing your life to the will of the fates. The tornado was starting to move and began to grow. I turned to Deacon. I could see the doubt and fear in his eyes. "Are you in or out?" I asked him.

Deacon's eyes were fixed on me, filled with concern and love. His voice quivered slightly as he uttered the words I feared the most. "I can't," he said, his voice tinged with a mixture of determination and desperation. "It's too dangerous, too unpredictable."

His words struck like a bolt of lightning. I stood there, torn between my love for the storm and my love for the man. It was a choice I never wanted to make. The man who had captured my heart and the storm that stirred my soul, each demanding my loyalty.

Silence hung in the air as we both grappled with the weight of the situation. In that moment, I realized the magnitude of my choice. With a heavy heart, I locked eyes with Deacon, taking a deep breath to steady myself. "I love you," I said, my voice filled with sincerity and longing.

With those words, I turned on my heel and hurried toward my SUV, the engine roaring to life as I ignited my own sense of adventure. I stole a final glance at Deacon standing in the driveway. In that moment, I knew I had left a part of my heart behind, but the storm has always been my true love. The engine roared to life as I sped towards the funnel cloud, the road disappearing beneath me in a blur of asphalt and determination.

The tires screeched as I accelerated, leaving a trail of dust and uncertainty in my wake. The storm loomed ever closer, its dark bands reaching out for me, making promises to me. My heart pounded in sync with the wipers on the SUV, creating a symphony of passion and reck-lessness.

I drove further into the storm's path, a wild embrace that matched the fury within my soul. In that moment I understood the price of my decision. There was no turning back. The thrill of the storm surged through me. It was a life force, igniting a fire that burned brighter than any love I had ever known. It was a lovers dance, a dance between danger and desire, the storm and me. It was a gamble that only the truly passionate would understand. And as the storm raged around me, I vowed to conquer it and to emerge unscathed.

Later that night, the world settled into an uneasy calm after the storm. Deacon prepared to go live from the scene, reporting on the aftermath of the storm. He began recounting the tale of the F5, the storm now a memory, saying it had been merciful, compared to storms in the past. He reported that there was only one casualty - a woman in an SUV - who was caught in the storm with no where to hide.

A pang of guilt tugged at his heart, and he couldn't shake the thought of what might have been. Deacon carried with him the weight of the storm, forever shaping his perspective. It was a reminder that life could change in an instant, that each moment was precious and should be cherished. It was also a reminder that sometimes, you have to throw your life to the winds.

Chapter Ten

LILY OF THE VALLEY

In the midst of the war's relentless chaos, I found myself navigating the treacherous landscape as a seasoned war correspondent, dedicated to capturing the truth and telling the untold stories of those caught in the crossfire. With a pen as my weapon, I ventured into the heart of danger, driven by a burning desire to shed light on the atrocities and inspire change. I found myself trapped within the walls of a city plagued by war. The once vibrant streets now lay in ruins, echoing with the sounds of gunfire and the cries of the wounded. Fear and despair clung to the air, suffocating any semblance of hope that remained.

My journey into the world of war reporting was not a path I had initially planned for. Raised in a small southern town, my childhood had been sheltered, filled with dreams of becoming a writer. But fate had other plans, and when the conflict broke out, I knew I couldn't stand idly by. Fueled by a restless spirit and an insatiable curiosity, I embarked on a journey that would forever change the course of my life.

As I delved deeper into war-torn cities and witnessed the unimaginable, a fire ignited within me, fueled by the stories of courage, resilience, and sacrifice that unfolded before my eyes. With every harrowing experience, I grew more determined to bear witness to the truth and share it with the world. Though haunted by the darkness I encountered, I remained resolute, driven by a deep-rooted belief that knowledge could be a catalyst for change. My words became a lifeline for those whose voices were silenced, and in the midst of the chaos, I found my purpose - to be the voice of the voiceless, shedding light on the untold stories of heroism amidst the horrors of war.

As I ventured into the heart of the war zone, the line between observer and participant blurred. The unpredictable nature of conflict soon caught up with me, and I found myself injured, caught in the crossfire of a battle I was merely there to document. I was whisked away to the nearest hospital, my body battered and my spirit shaken. It was there, lying on a sterile hospital bed, that I first met her – a young nurse named Lily, whose gentle touch and unwavering compassion soothed the pain that ravaged my body and soul. With her bright green eyes and a smile that could light up the darkest of rooms, she exuded a quiet strength that mirrored the resilience of the war-torn city.

In her presence, I found calm amidst the chaos, and as she tended to my wounds, I couldn't help but feel a stirring connection, a glimpse of something deeper that transcended the confines of our respective roles. Lily had experienced her own share of heartache and loss, her life in this city had been marked by tragedy that could have broken anyone's spirit. But instead of succumbing to despair, she channeled her pain into a deep reservoir of empathy, using her skills as a nurse to bring healing to those in need. Her gentle touch, soothing voice, and unwavering dedication offered a glimmer of hope to the broken souls who found themselves within the walls of the makeshift hospital.

Her past had molded her into the courageous woman she had become. The loss of her family in a previous conflict had ignited a fire within her, a burning desire to alleviate suffering and bring light to the darkest of times. Her unwavering resolve to make a difference, to bring humanity amidst the chaos, was a testament to the depth of her character. Lily was a beacon of hope in a world marred by destruction, and her strength and selflessness would forever be etched in my heart.

In the shadows of what remained of the ghostly buildings, we stole moments and paused, sharing our dreams and fears. Lily revealed her own stories of loss and sacrifice, yet she never let bitterness consume her heart. As soldiers often do in trenches, we found our bond grew stronger with every danger we faced. Together, we navigated hazardous paths, evading gunfire and dodging collapsing structures. We saw the worst of humanity, but also witnessed small acts of bravery and kindness that reminded us of the power of love.

As the days turned into weeks, Lily and I began to find a peacefulness in each other's company. I found it odd, being surrounded by so much death and destruction I could actually find myself falling in love with this lily of the war-torn valley. Our connection grew stronger with every shared moment, our hearts entwined in a dance of longing and desire. In stolen moments, we searched for the private sanctuary we created within each other's arms, finding comfort and warmth amidst the confusion of this troubled land. Never knowing if this day would be our last, we decided to live each day to the fullest. We laughed, we cried, and we shared our dreams and fears, building a bond that defied the darkness surrounding us.

It was amidst the disharmony of destruction that our love was tested, and yet it flourished, fueled by a passion that burned brighter with every passing day. As bombs fell around us, their explosions serving as a haunting backdrop of mortality, we found ourselves drawn closer, seeking alleviation in the midst of the chaos. In one unforgettable moment, with the deafening sounds of war echoing in our ears, our lips met in a kiss that spoke volumes of our love and defiance. The war stood still as we melted into each other's embrace, our hearts pounding in sync with the rhythm of the world falling apart.

In the heart of a bombed-out building, with the remnants of shattered walls surrounding us, Lily and I shared a moment that defied the chaos and destruction. As sirens wailed in the distance, their cries blending with the symphony of falling debris, our lips met in a fervent kiss. Time stood still as the world faded away, leaving only the intoxicating taste of our love on our lips. In that moment, the power of our connection engulfed us, drowning out the screams of war and filling the void with an overwhelming sense of belonging.

The scent of war hung heavy in the air, mingling with the acrid smoke and the lingering aroma of fear. But amidst the bitterness, there was a sweet undercurrent of love and hope. As we held each other close, our bodies pressed together against a standing wall and in a dance of desire, the scent of Lily's perfume intertwined with the essence of determination and resilience. Lily's perfume was an enchanting elixir. It grounded her to humanity and to what life once was. Amidst the chaos, each delicate note, whispered of her essence, infusing the air with the scent of blooming roses and warm vanilla. Inhaling its intoxicating fragrance, I was transported to a realm where love conquered all, where beauty transcended the desolation that surrounded us.

Her perfume became a symbol of hope and a tangible reminder of our connection, a sign of the tenderness and passion that bound our hearts together. In our embrace, we found a reminder that even in the midst of war, love could be a sanctuary, a haven where our souls could mingle and find refuge from the storms that raged against humanity. Our love became an antidote to the horrors surrounding us, a fragrant oasis in the midst of the desolation. In that abandoned building, we found comfort in each other's arms, defying the darkness with a love that bloomed against all odds.

We treasured each stolen glance, every touch, as if it were a precious gem, for we knew that our time together was uncertain and fragile. Through whispered words and tender caresses, we vowed to hold onto each other fiercely, to let love guide us through the darkest of times. Together, we navigated the treacherous paths, finding strength in each other, and finding comfort in the knowledge that, no matter what the world threw at us, our love would always endure, a beacon of light fighting against the chaos of war.

The next day the town was eerily quiet and I wondered

if the fighting was over. My captain ordered me to follow along and get a first hand account of the war. It seemed safe. I was hesitant, not wanting to leave Lily, but I had my orders and I left with the morning light.

Walking through the remnants of the once-thriving city, the destruction was a haunting tableau of shattered dreams and broken promises. Crumbling buildings stood as silent witnesses to the horrors that had unfolded, their jagged edges reaching toward the heavens in a desperate plea for redemption. Dust settled like a heavy shroud, casting a grey pallor over the remnants of a vibrant civilization. I couldn't shake the feeling that this eerie stillness was merely a reprieve, a deceptive lull before the storm. The scars of battle whispered of a conflict far from over, and the heaviness in the air seemed to bear the weight of impending darkness.

As I navigated the treacherous streets, shadows danced along the broken pavement, casting eerie silhouettes that seemed to echo the cries of the fallen. Our steps faltered, our gazes tracing the destruction that surrounded us. The echo of distant gunfire served as a chilling reminder that danger lurked just beyond the horizon. We were warned to return before darkness overtook the city. In the cloak of night, the streets transformed into a treacherous labyrinth where survival was a constant battle.

Whispers of hope were carried on the wind, a delicate

melody amidst the sea of destruction. We pressed on, my spirits unyielding, my heart refusing to be overshadowed by despair. With each step, I found my sense of purpose again. The stories of the fallen were screaming to be told. My unit quietly turned and began their journey back, preparing for what was to be a turning point in the war.

In the pitch-black night, chaos descended upon the city in a violent symphony of destruction. The deafening roar of bombs filled the air, shaking the ground beneath us. With terror gripping our hearts, we sought refuge deep in the makeshift hospital, praying that its fragile walls would shield us from the storm of devastation. As the bombs fell, shards of glass shattered and debris rained down around us, but Lily, with her unwavering determination, refused to abandon her post. Amidst the smoke and flickering lights, she tirelessly tended to the wounded, her hands steady and her eyes filled with a resolve that defied the terror that threatened to engulf us.

Fear took hold of me as the storm of destruction intensified. In the swirling confusion, I lost sight of Lily amidst the debris and the cries of anguish. Panic surged through my veins as I searched desperately, calling out her name amidst the rubble. The scent of smoke and burning remains suffocated my senses, and my heart ached with the fear of losing her. Every passing second felt like an eternity as I navigated through the wreckage, praying to reunite with the woman who had become my anchor in this unforgiving world.

The devastation was overwhelming, the aftermath of the raid painting a grim portrait of destruction. The hospital, once a sanctuary, now bore the scars of war. But amidst the ruins, the indomitable spirit of Lily persisted. I knew she would defy the chaos that threatened to consume us all. The thought of her resilience ignited a fire within me, propelling me forward through the debris, my determination to find her eclipsing the fear that clung to my every step.

Finally, as the smoke began to clear, our eyes met across the remnants of what was once a place of healing. Relief washed over me as I rushed into her embrace. Holding her tightly I breathed in her perfume. I realized what I was feeling truly was love for this woman. Her love was the only thing keeping me grounded in a world turned upside down. In that moment, the horrors of the night faded into insignificance as the strength of our love triumphed over the darkness that threatened to tear us apart. In that moment, I knew I wanted to take her and run, run from the horrors of war, forgetting everything we knew and forgetting everything we had seen.

We emerged from the chaos, scarred but unbroken. The night raid tested the depths of our resolve and solidified our bond. In the face of terror and uncertainty, we had found each other, our love a guiding light amidst the shadows. Together we were fueled by the knowledge that even amidst the ruins, love could still bloom. In that darkened moment, we both knew we had survived. Amidst the rubble, we promised to hold onto each other fiercely, to never let the darkness extinguish the light that burned within us.

In a fleeting moment, as we stood amidst the chaos, Lily's lips met mine in a tender kiss that spoke volumes of our love and the uncertainty that engulfed us. But even as the warmth of her touch lingered on my lips, duty called her away. With a whispered promise to return, Lily looked deeply into my eyes, her green eyes shining through the darkness. She rested her hand on my cheek, reached up and kissed my forehead and whispered, "I love you, now and always". She gracefully moved across the room to tend to someone in desperate need of her care. My heart swelled with admiration for her selflessness, even as a knot of worry tightened in my chest.

Time stretched in suspended anticipation as Lily's figure receded into the distance, her determined steps a testament to her unwavering dedication. She turned back to smile at me, raised her hand and blew an invisible kiss. Lily simultaneously raised her foot and stepped backwards, stepping on an unexploded bomb. The bomb unleashed its devastating power. The force of the explosion tore through the air, shattering what remained of the fragile sanctuary we had sought. The shockwave reverberated through the walls, an indiscriminate force that mercilessly separated us within the fractured structure.

I frantically called out Lily's name, my voice lost in the chaos that surrounded us. The dust-filled air obscured my vision, each step forward a treacherous dance through the debris. The building had become a labyrinth, its walls a maze of uncertainty. I searched desperately, my heart pounding in my chest, praying that Lily was alive amidst the wreckage, praying that fate would grant us another chance to be reunited in the aftermath of this cataclysmic event. In the chaos and smoke, I searched frantically for Lily, praying that she had survived.

Finally, I found her, bloodied and broken, yet her spirit remained unyielding. I held her closely and watched as she slipped from this life. With tears streaming down my face, I held her in my arms, whispering words of love and gratitude. In that moment, as the war raged around us, I understood the true meaning of sacrifice. Lily, my love, lay lifeless in my arms, her spirit extinguished by the merciless blast. The world around me faded into insignificance as my soul was ripped from my body, consumed by an agonizing grief that threatened to engulf me entirely. I clung to her lifeless form, whispering words of love and anguish, unable to comprehend the cruel twist of fate that had torn her from my embrace.

Amidst my misery, my unit came rushing through the chaos, their urgent voices forcing me to leave Lily's side. Reluctantly, I tore myself away from her, my heart shattered into a million irreparable fragments. The city had fallen to the insurgents, its streets now under the control of those who sought to spread nothing but destruction and despair. I was forced to retreat, leaving behind the shattered remnants of our hopes and dreams, and a love that had sustained us in the darkest of times.

I'm not sure how many days and nights passed; I was catatonic. Life was a blur to me, I was in shock and denial. I received my orders after returning to base. I was being sent home, being returned to a world that had moved on, oblivious to the scars etched upon my soul. But I could not escape the haunting specter of Lily's love. Her presence lingered in every corner, her laughter echoing in my dreams, her touch a bittersweet phantom upon my skin. The nights became a solitary torment, haunted by the memories we had shared, the promises left unfulfilled. Lily had become an ethereal presence, an eternal flame within my heart, guiding me through the emptiness that had now overpowered my existence.

In the depths of my grief, I vowed to honor Lily's memory, to carry her love as the light through the darkness that threatened to consume me. The war had taken so much, but it could not extinguish the flame of love that burned within. And so, I forged ahead, a wounded soul carrying the weight of loss, determined to find meaning in a world forever changed.

* * *

Thank you for reading.
Look for the next book in the series:
LOVE ENCOUNTERS, VOLUME 2
Releasing soon.

About the Author

Born and raised just outside of Atlanta, Emily is a self proclaimed caffeine addict, connoisseur of inexpensive wine, and lover of books. In addition to being all of these things, she's first and foremost a wife and mom.

Growing up, she shared her grandmother's love of reading. But where she leaned toward murder mysteries, Emily was obsessed with all things love and romance.

When she's not nose deep in her next manuscript, or binging sit-coms, you can usually find her with a book in hand.

Also by Emily Edwards

VOLUME 2

love
ENCOUNTERS

SULTRY TALES OF LOVE & PASSION

EMILY EDWARDS

Also by Free Reign Publishing